THE ROBIN HOOD OF THE RANGE

Ricky Cates is a vicious outlaw who kills without remorse. He also has a talent for deception, having convinced a local writer that he's the Robin Hood of the Range: a man who takes from the rich and gives to the poor. Rance Dehner is on Cates's blood-spattered trail. But before he can reach his target, he must confront Cates's henchmen, another detective obsessed with catching the killer — and a young woman who is hopelessly and dangerously in love with this Robin Hood . . .

N

JAMES CLAY

THE ROBIN HOOD OF THE RANGE

Complete and Unabridged

LINFORD
Leicester

First published in Great Britain in 2015 by
Robert Hale Limited
London

First Linford Edition
published 2017
by arrangement with
Robert Hale
an imprint of
The Crowood Press
Wiltshire

A catalogue record for this book is available
from the British Library.

ISBN 978–1–4448–3308–9

Published by
F. A. Thorpe (Publishing)
Anstey, Leicestershire

Set by Words & Graphics Ltd.
Anstey, Leicestershire
Printed and bound in Great Britain by
T. J. International Ltd., Padstow, Cornwall

This book is printed on acid-free paper

1

Rance Dehner peered cautiously over the top of a thick bush. He was on a rocky slope, and one misstep could cause him to fall and be captured. He watched as four horsemen wove their mounts among the large stone outcroppings and scraggly trees and down to the road at the bottom. Two of the men dismounted, took ropes off their saddles and walked back up the hill a few feet. A tree was lying there. Dehner had watched them cut it down the previous day.

Each of the two men tied a rope around the tree and tied the other end of the rope to the horns of their saddles. The remaining two men kept watch as they pulled the thorny locust tree across the road where it would block the stagecoach, which was due by in an hour or so. One of the oldest tricks in the book, Dehner thought. He was obviously dealing with novices. That wasn't necessarily good. An amateur tends to go for his gun quicker than a professional thief who is armed with a slew of tricks to escape the law.

Dehner was a detective for the Lowrie Agency. Three weeks before, he had captured a young bandit who had robbed a Wells Fargo stage depot. The kid's name was Jamie Everett. He was scared, remorseful and very talkative. He admitted to being part of a gang that had robbed a stagecoach three months back. Jamie informed the law that the gang was planning to regroup and pull another job soon. He provided all the information he could, mostly relating to where the gang was to meet. The details of the robbery were to be given to the crooks by the leader, a guy who called himself Ricky Cates.

The law in that section of Arizona was spread thin, so Wells Fargo had hired the Lowrie Agency to stop the robbery and apprehend the gang. They weren't too fussy on that last point. The folks at the stagecoach line wanted the gang stopped. How that was done was up to Dehner and Sam Wilcock, another detective from the Lowrie Agency. This was a two man job.

Dehner kept the bush between himself and the robbers as they rode back up to the top of the hill. Sam Wilcock was somewhere on the other side of the hill. The plan was to let the robbers stop the stagecoach. While they were grouped close together and focused on the stage, the two detectives would come up on them from behind. Hopefully, they would surrender without a fight.

Nothing much happened for an hour. Then Dehner saw one of the four men at the top of the hill point down the road. He must have spotted a moving cloud of dust from the oncoming stage. The men pulled bandannas over their faces. They rode about halfway down the hill and waited. Dehner crept away from the bush to where he had tethered his horse behind jutting boulders. He mounted his bay as the stagecoach clattered to a stop.

Two of the four outlaws fired shots into the air and all of them surrounded the coach, ordering the shotgun to drop his weapon. One of the robbers fired a shot over the head of the shotgun to ensure that the man got the point. He did. As the Winchester dropped to the ground, a female passenger inside the coach screamed.

All the commotion made it easy for Dehner and his partner to meet together on the slope. Sam Wilcock was riding a sorrel. He was a heavyset man, balding, a few years short of forty, with a moon face dominated by intense, probing eyes.

Wilcock showed Dehner the palm of his hand, indicating they were to remain where they were for the moment. Dehner followed the silent order. Technically, the two men had equal stature in the agency. But Wilcock was older than Rance and had a reputation throughout the west for his toughness and success as a detective. Rance had allowed Wilcock to be the boss of this operation, as he had on previous occasions when they worked together. So far, Sam Wilcock had given him no reason to regret the arrangement.

'Everyone out! Don't try nothin' funny!'

The two detectives watched as three passengers exited the stagecoach: an older man and his wife, and a man carrying a black medical bag who was obviously a doctor. One of the robbers quickly dismounted with a sack in his hand. He shouted threats at the passengers as he ordered them to drop all their valuables into the brown flour sack. The crook's last stop was the doctor. After taking the doc's wallet, he grabbed the medical bag, opened it, and apparently not finding anything inside that looked valuable, shoved the black bag into the chest of the doctor, who grabbed it before it fell.

'Back inside!' All three people scurried back into the coach.

The gunman on foot yelled at the driver, 'Throw down the strongbox!'

The driver complied. The box had barely hit the ground when the outlaw who had shouted the orders put a bullet into the lock. Then, tossing the flour sack to the ground, he yanked the lock off and opened the box.

'We done good, boys!' he exclaimed gleefully as he took large saddle-bags off his horse and began to fill them up with money from the strongbox.

What happened next put a smile on the face of Sam Wilcock. The three other outlaws rode up to the strongbox, where they could watch their colleague stuff the money into his saddle-bags. All four outlaws were now huddled together as Wilcock had predicted they would be.

The two detectives spurred their horses and rode into view with their weapons drawn.

'Drop your guns, right now!' Wilcock's voice boomed. Rance noticed his colleague's voice alone seemed to startle the outlaws into obedience. They did what they were told. 'Now, get down off them horses!' The three robbers on horseback dismounted.

Rance rode to one side of the outlaws near the front of the stagecoach and Wilcock guided his horse until it stopped beside the back end of the coach. They had the four robbers covered. Dehner started to get off his horse to collect the guns which were now lying on the ground. Standard procedure. But he stopped when Sam yelled, 'Give me those saddle-bags — now!'

The robber who had relieved the passengers of their valuables tossed the saddle-bags at Sam Wilcock. Wilcock removed his right foot from the stirrup of his saddle and reached leftward to catch the bag. He fell off his horse, firing his Remington as he hit the ground. Everyone ducked down, not knowing where the bullet was headed.

Wilcock's horse panicked, wheeled around and began to run, dragging Wilcock, whose foot was still in the stirrup of his saddle. Dehner holstered his Colt and rode after the sorrel, catching up to the animal and stopping it after it had run only a short distance.

Dehner had to duck again to avoid another shot, this one coming from the outlaws. All four robbers were back on their horses. They had jumped the tree and were riding off. Rance drew his

Colt and returned fire. During the quick volley of shots he heard a cry of pain. From the corner of his eye he saw the shotgun clutching his shoulder as he climbed unsteadily from the stagecoach and crumpled to the ground.

The outlaws were riding fast and out of gun range. Dehner looked toward Sam Wilcock, who had freed his left foot and was now getting up. Rance rode back to the stagecoach and dismounted.

The passengers were leaving the coach. First out was the doctor, a lean man in his thirties, who ran to the shotgun and crouched over the injured man seconds before Rance got there.

'Take it easy, Lou,' the doctor spoke to the shotgun, then looked at the driver. 'What happened, Charlie? I thought Lou tossed down his rifle.'

'He did,' the driver replied. 'But he kept a pistol behind the seat. He used it to fire at those jaspers after that fool fell off his horse.'

Charlie, a grey-bearded man, looked at Rance. 'Who are you fellas, anyhow?'

Rance Dehner looked around. All the passengers were now gathered around Lou and it seemed that everyone, even the injured shotgun, was looking his way. Well, maybe not exactly his way. There was obviously a great deal of interest in Sam Wilcock, whom Dehner could hear approaching from behind.

Dehner waited until Wilcock stood beside him. 'We're detectives from the Lowrie Agency. We were hired to prevent that gang of outlaws from robbing — '

'Great job you did,' Lou grunted from where he lay injured.

'Take it easy,' the doctor cautioned.

'Lou is right!' the coach's only woman passenger spoke as she looked accusingly at Sam Wilcock. 'Some detective you are! You can't even stay on your horse!'

The woman's husband began to laugh, exposing the fact that he didn't have many teeth. 'Why don't ya come inta town with us, Mr Detective? The fella who owns the livery sometimes gives riding lessons. Right now, he's teaching my grandson. He's seven years old. After

9

a few weeks, maybe you could be as good as him.'

Laughter followed; Rance noticed that even Lou was chuckling. Maybe the cruel joke served a good purpose.

Sam Wilcock disagreed. 'It ain't funny!'

'Guess it ain't so funny,' Charlie was still crouched over the wounded shotgun. 'You almost got a man killed and that gang made off with one thousand two hundred dollars. I don't think that there agency of yours is gonna get any more jobs from Wells Fargo.'

Sam Wilcock looked down at the wounded man, a range of emotions on his face. His lips moved for a moment but no words came out. He then turned away with a look of shame.

Dehner tried to diffuse the tenseness in the air. 'Doc, can we get Lou into town?'

'In a few minutes, yes,' the doctor continued, wrapping a tight bandage on the wound. 'The bullet winged him, but I don't think it did any major damage. As soon as I get the bleeding stopped, we'll get him into the coach. I can ride up front.'

Lou looked at the travellers who surrounded him. 'See what that fool detective did? Now our sawbones is gonna get his own bones rattled good while he has to listen to Charlie's corny jokes.'

While most of the group laughed, Sam Wilcock walked briskly back to his horse. Dehner followed him. 'Where are you going, Sam?'

'Where do you think? After that gang of outlaws!'

Wilcock's voice was angry. Dehner tried to sound calm and reasonable. 'First, I think we should move that locust tree so the stage — '

'And let people laugh at me some more about how I should take riding lessons with a seven-year-old!' When Wilcock reached his sorrel, he turned and faced Dehner. 'I'm recovering that money and I'm bringing back those four snakes. Dead. We'll see who's laughing then!'

'Sam ... '

Wilcock didn't want to hear any more. He mounted his horse.

'As soon as that tree is out of the road, I'll join you, we —'

'Suit yourself!' Wilcock spurred his horse into a fast gallop.

Working alone, Dehner managed to get the tree moved at about the same time Lou was ready to board the stage. The detective said farewell to Charlie and his passengers and then headed out after the outlaws. But as he followed the trail, a nervous feeling pricked at him.

Dehner couldn't help but feel that the most dangerous of the men he was pursuing was Sam Wilcock.

2

The trail was easy to follow. About a thirty minute ride from where the stagecoach had been held up was a stream, one of the few sources of water in the area. The crooks would almost have to head there in order to refresh their horses.

Dehner examined the footprints and markings around the stream carefully before letting his own horse walk over the marks to drink. What he saw didn't surprise him. The outlaws appeared to have used the time to divide up the money and go their own ways.

The detective had no trouble spotting the separate set of hoof prints that went after one of the robbers. Why Sam Wilcock had chosen this particular crook, Dehner didn't know, and he didn't pause very long to think about it.

As he followed the trail, Dehner mused on why Sam Wilcock had been so enraged by the mockery he received from the group back at the scene of the robbery. Part of it had to be that Wilcock was angry with himself. Sam's carelessness got a man shot and allowed the robbers to escape with the loot.

Those blunders were not typical of Sam Wilcock. He was a first rate detective. But was he anything else? Dehner had never heard Wilcock make reference to a family or even friends. He seemed to have no life outside of his job.

Maybe that was the problem.

Dehner's sense of unease grew stronger. What life did *he* have except for being a detective?

As it often did when he was riding alone, that horrible day came back to him: the day when the woman he loved died because of his carelessness. Dehner's life was now dedicated to doing penance, to somehow making up for the irredeemable loss of that day. He knew the task was impossible, but he also knew it was the only life he could live.

And he wondered if Sam Wilcock was

battling a similar demon.

Voices sounded from a distance but Dehner couldn't discern what they were saying. He halted his bay and listened. One voice was high pitched, almost pleading. It seemed to be coming from the other side of a large, horseshoe shaped knoll to his right.

Dehner rode to the far end of the knoll. He collected a few large stones and used them to anchor his horse's reins securely to the ground. He hoped that would be enough. There could be gunplay. The detective didn't want his horse running off. He patted the bay, then walked cautiously to the side of the knoll and peered around.

Sam Wilcock was looking in Dehner's direction but didn't see him. The older detective was glaring intensely at a man who, by his clothes, Dehner recognized from the robbery. The outlaw's back was to Dehner. The beginnings of a campfire lay between the robber and Sam Wilcock. The cocky, inexperienced outlaw had set up camp early.

The crook held his hands shoulder high. Those hands moved about in a beseeching manner. 'Look, ya can have it all, three hundred dollars. That's pretty good money. Take it. Please!'

'I don't accept bribes, Allan,' came Wilcock's cold reply. 'I'm no cheap thug, like you.'

'OK, then, OK. Arrest me.'

Wilcock's voice boomed as it had when he first confronted the outlaws during the hold-up. 'So, you're gonna surrender to a man at least fifteen years older than you. I figured you for a yellow snake ... a coward.'

Allan's voice trembled, as did his body. 'I know what you're trying to do. It ain't gonna work. Ya can't prod me inta trying to outdraw ya. I ain't falling for it.'

'Yes, you will, Allan.' Wilcock coughed out a low rumble that may have been a laugh. 'Every man has a breaking point. That rule even goes for a worthless mama's boy like you.'

'Ya shouldn't —'

Whatever Allan was going to say next,

got cut off. Dehner stepped out from behind the side of the knoll. 'The man has surrendered, Sam. Take his gun.'

Anger and confusion flashed across Wilcock's face. 'Stay outta this, Rance. It don't concern you, it's none of your business.'

Dehner's right hand hovered over his Colt .45. 'That's not true, Sam. This is very much my business. I'm going to take this stupid kid to a jail cell and stop you from doing something you'll regret the rest of your life.'

Dehner had intentionally called the robber a kid. He hoped the outlaw's youth and obvious inexperience would stay Sam Wilcock's hand.

Wilcock became stone. His eyes remained fixed on the outlaw.

Allan nervously turned his head around to Dehner. 'Please, mister, take my gun. I'd hand it to ya, but he'll kill me the moment I reach down. So, take my gun right outta its holster. I ain't gonna try no tricks. Promise.'

Wilcock's voice boomed once again.

'Stay right where you are, Rance!'

'I'm taking this man prisoner, Sam.'

Dehner felt trapped in the lowest pit of hell. Would he actually have to draw on Sam Wilcock? If it came to that, he knew he would have to kill Wilcock. His fellow detective would be a very dangerous man if wounded.

Of course, Rance thought, all that assumes I would be faster than Sam Wilcock, which is far from a sure bet.

Dehner was focused on Wilcock's face which was now a blank slate. In the periphery of his vision, he watched Allan, a terrified young thief, who might panic and try something foolish.

Rance didn't see the figure that stepped out from the other end of the knoll. 'Sorry to interrupt this little family squabble, gents. But I ain't got time to listen to two jaspers argue 'fore they kill each other. You're takin' up too much of my valuable time; guess I'll jus' have to do the killin' myself.'

'Ricky Cates!' Allan shouted. 'I'm sure glad to see you!'

Cates was a tall, angular man with blondish-brown hair. His Buffalo Bill style hair and beard showed signs of meticulous care. Cates's boots were expensive as was the pearl handled six-gun in his right hand. He stood several yards behind Sam Wilcock, who had to look backwards in order to see the intruder.

Ricky ignored Allan's joyful greeting and spoke to the detectives. 'Drop your guns, both of you. Nothin' funny.'

Cates was going to shoot them down in cold blood, Dehner was sure of that. With a few bullets, the leader of the outlaw band could eliminate two pesky detectives.

Rance decided to try, in Cates's word, something 'funny'. Instead of dropping his gun, he tossed it away in a shaky gesture. The gun landed behind the knoll but still within the detective's sight.

The move pleased Cates, who believed Dehner was scared to the point of shaking and without a gun, harmless. He turned his attention to Sam Wilcock who had dropped his .44 immediately beside him.

'Turn around, I wanna see your ugly face.'

Wilcock did what he was told.

Cates shifted his attention to Allan. 'Where's the money? Your cut.'

Allan pointed downwards to where his saddle and saddle-bags lay on the ground. 'Right there.'

Cates made a beckoning gesture with his left hand. 'Bring it here.'

'My horse is over in that grove of trees, Ricky. It'll only take me a few minutes to saddle up and — '

'I said bring it here!'

The young outlaw nodded his head anxiously, picked up his saddle-bags and began to carry them to Ricky Cates. Allan didn't know what was coming next. Rance did. The detective took two running steps toward the knoll then jumped behind it as a bullet from Cates's gun speared into the knoll, cutting far into the dirt.

Dehner now had cover. Allan and Sam did not. Dehner had no time to aim. He grabbed his Colt, did a fast belly crawl to where he could see his target and sent a shot in Ricky Cates's direction.

Dehner missed but the bullet whistled near Cates, forcing him to flop down on his stomach. The killer squeezed off a shot toward Sam Wilcock, who was starting to pick up his .44. The bullet spurted dust on the bottom of Wilcock's pants leg. The detective danced backwards, stumbled and fell but wasn't hurt.

Cates was in trouble but spotted his escape. Allan stood nearby, rendered immobile by the chaos around him. He looked towards Cates like a boy beckoning his big brother for protection from school-yard bullies. Ricky Cates fired two hot flames into the young outlaw. Allan screamed and yelled as he collapsed to the ground. Dehner couldn't decipher Allan's words but they resounded with a shocked betrayal.

With panther speed, Cates rose to his feet, darted toward the saddle-bags Allan had dropped, scooped them up and ran for his horse. Wilcock buoyed up and got off a wayward shot at Cates. Confident that Ricky Cates was no longer a threat, Sam moved toward Allan. As Dehner ran toward the fallen outlaw he could hear the sound of hoof beats.

Both detectives crouched over Allan. Blood bubbled from his mouth as he tried to speak.

'Why ... '

'Don't try to talk,' Wilcock ordered. 'We're gonna fix you up.'

'Why would Ricky do ... he was friend, good friend.'

'Some friend,' Wilcock snapped as he examined the outlaw's wounds. 'He shot you, so he could take the money.'

Allan's voice was becoming a gurgle. 'I woulda give him money ... '

'Ricky knew if he shot you there was a good chance Sam and I would stay around and patch you up,' Dehner said.

'That allowed him to ride off.'

Allan's face was becoming increasingly pale and empty. But he still seemed able to understand what Dehner had said. 'Guess I got a lot to learn 'bout life.'

Those words startled Sam Wilcock.

He turned his head away. When his face was again visible, Dehner could see it was contorting. 'Yes, you got a lot to learn about life, I guess we all do.'

Allan seemed to lose all sense of time and place as more blood oozed from his mouth. The young man began to moan in a sing-song manner, occasionally pronouncing a word, or trying to.

Dehner whispered to his partner, 'The bullet near the heart looks like it's deep. Very deep. I've pried bullets out of a man before but I've never pulled out anything that far inside.'

'I have,' Wilcock replied. He used his head as a pointer. 'My horse is tied over there to a bush. I carry two sets of saddle-bags. One big, one small. Bring me the small one. Got a knife and a few other tools in there. Bring it to me, along with the canteen.'

'Right.' Dehner ran to Wilcock's sorrel, retrieved the saddle-bags and canteen, then ran back. When he returned, Sam Wilcock was on his feet, staring at the body on the ground.

'We won't be needing any of that stuff.' Sam swiped a hand over his forehead. 'Just two shovels.'

'I'll return the saddle-bags,' Dehner said. This time Rance walked slowly to the sorrel and back. Sam Wilcock needed some time alone.

3

They buried the young man. Wilcock spoke softly as they dug.

'He started off trying to be my friend, you know how some captured outlaws act. Never got around to saying his last name.'

After the body was buried, Dehner read a psalm and said a brief prayer. The two detectives then finished building the fire Allan had started. Supper was a silent affair. Not until they were on their second cup of coffee did Sam begin to talk.

'The kid had a good horse. I know this area well. A lot of hardscrabble outfits around here. There's one less than a half mile. Nice folks. Young couple with a kid. They fed me a great meal a year or so back, when I stopped to ask questions about an owl hoot I was after. Why don't we take the horse there first thing in the morning? I'm sure they could make good

25

use of it. We won't lose much time.'

'Sure.'

'There's no reason we can't do something nice to help people.' Sam Wilcock spoke as if Dehner, or someone, was arguing the matter with him. 'We don't always have to be doing things because it's our job.'

'Sure.'

Sam looked upwards into the dark night. One star was visible but its light appeared to flicker as if it was going out. 'Something the kid said sorta got to me.'

Dehner's reply wasn't really a question. 'You mean that remark about having a lot to learn about life?'

'Yep. How many cases have we worked together on, Rance?'

'Ah … this one is our third.'

'I'm glad I work alone, most of the time. Like it that way. Know you feel the same. But when I hafta work with someone else, you're the best partner a man could ask for, Rance. I guess you're the closest thing I got to a friend.' Wilcock's face scrunched up as if there were something wrong in his life, but he couldn't identify it. 'You know what it's like being a detective.'

Sam Wilcock was trying to work something out. All Dehner could do was provide a friendly ear. 'Yes.'

'People call you all kinds of stuff. I'm older than you, Rance, I've probably been called names even you haven't heard.'

'Probably,' Rance agreed.

'None of that bothered me,' Wilcock continued. 'But back at the stagecoach hold-up, when people laughed at me, I went a bit crazy, a lot crazy, I guess.'

'Being laughed at is different than being called names, Sam.'

Wilcock bobbed his head in agreement. 'But it was my own damn fault. I made a stupid mistake. I got an innocent man shot and allowed dangerous outlaws to escape. One of them, Ricky Cates, is a brutal killer ... and we had them captured ... I felt proud because my plan had worked and then I got careless ... I deserved to be laughed it ... I can't blame those folks ... '

'Life humiliates all of us at times, Sam. We have to live with that.'

Sam Wilcock paused, as if considering what his partner had just said. When he spoke again his voice was filled with remorse. 'I need to thank you. What you said a while back was right. If I had goaded that kid into a gunfight I never could have lived with myself. Thanks, Rance.'

'No thanks needed. You would have come to your senses. You wouldn't have prodded Allan into a fight you know he couldn't have won.'

'I wish I could be sure of that.' Wilcock looked back up into the sky. The star was gone. 'Guess we should turn in. We got an early day tomorrow and a tough one.'

'You're right.'

They turned in, but Dehner reckoned Sam Wilcock would get little sleep on this night.

4

Andy Nolan stopped at a familiar tree and slid off his horse. He was both exhausted and shaken. How could he have allowed Ricky Cates to talk him into such a dangerous thing? They had almost been caught. If that lawman hadn't taken a tumble, the whole bunch of them would be in jail right now.

How would he have explained that to Priscilla?

Restless clouds battled a sliver of a moon which could toss only an occasional, scant light through the branches of the forest. Andy had to light a match to make sure he was at the right tree. Yes, he was in the right place. He could read the letters. He had carved those letters the first day he and Priscilla had started the ranch. 'AN LUVS PN' all contained within a heart. Corny, but Priscilla loved it. The two of them occasionally strolled out to this tree on pleasant evenings.

Now Andy felt he was committing a sacrilege, burying stolen money under this special tree. But it was the only place where the money would be safe and easy to find. After burying the money, he felt a need to pray. He wanted to ask God to let him get away with theft just this one time. He'd use the money to settle matters with the bank and buy a few things the ranch desperately needed.

'I don't think the Lord would take too kindly to that,' Andy whispered to himself as he mounted his horse. 'I just hope Pris never finds out what I done.'

As his tired horse shuffled toward home, Nolan thought about the shotgun who had taken a bullet and wondered if he had died. Andy hadn't fired a shot during the entire robbery, but he knew enough about the law to know just being in the gang responsible for a killing could get him hanged.

On most occasions like this, Andy would run into the house and hug Priscilla before attending to his horse.

But on this night, he headed directly for the barn. He didn't want his wife to see how hard the animal had been ridden.

As he walked from the barn to the small ranch house, he could see his wife standing in the doorway, a dark silhouette against a flickering kerosene yellow. As he embraced her everything seemed fine, for a few precious seconds.

Priscilla broke away from him a little too quickly. 'Are you hungry?'

'Nah, I don't need no grub.'

They stepped into the house together. 'How did the meeting with Mr Collins go?'

There was something wrong in Priscilla's voice but he didn't know what.

'Went just fine!' he lifted both hands as he spoke. 'The man made me a great offer. Why, we're gonna be able to pay what we owe to the bank and — '

'Is Mr Collins a nice man?'

Andy sensed more unease in his wife but tried to maintain the happy facade. 'Ah, yes, sure, a real fine man.'

'Is he as nice as Mr Smith?'

'Whaddya mean?'

'When you left here three days ago, it was about an important business meeting with Mr Smith. You're a terrible liar, Andy! Where have you been?'

Andy Nolan looked into his wife's pretty face, now contorted by anger and ... what else? Was she disillusioned with him and their life together? Did she wish she had married Paul Carnes instead of him?

Andy felt angry and ashamed. Not knowing what else to do, he yelled at Priscilla, 'I'm doing everything I can for us, and you go rawhiding me for — '

'Is lying the best you can do?!'

The young husband wanted to break down and cry, tell his wife everything he had done and beg her forgiveness. But he couldn't do that.

'I'm tired. I'm getting some sleep.' He stormed out of the house and walked toward the barn, hoping Priscilla would come after him. She didn't.

The hay in the barn was comfortable enough, but he slept lightly and only because he was exhausted. Andy's sleep was punctuated with vivid images of the shotgun falling from the stagecoach, his dreams being more bloody and gruesome than what he had actually seen from a distance.

As the sky turned red, Andy gave up on sleep and began to walk around the inside of the barn. He thought about that day only a little more than a month back when his life took a terrible turn. He had just purchased supplies from Womack's General Store when the owner, Carl Womack, began to work both of his hands on the counter as if he were playing the piano.

'Andy, today is the end unless you do something.'

'I don't follow you.'

Carl Womack twitched nervously. He was a middle-aged man with a brown beard who had served in the army. But his military bearing was as tattered as the old tunic he kept in a closet and wore on the fourth of July.

'I can't give you any more credit, until

you pay me. Now, you don't have to pay off the whole account, just twenty-five per cent would be all right ... or something close to it.'

'I can't pay you that soon, Carl. You know what things are like right now. But I'm gonna pay you back, I'm an honest man, you know that!'

'Of course, I know all that, but ... well ... I've got bills to pay, too. And you're running up a huge tab. I'm sorry, Andy, I really am.'

'Sure.' Andy Nolan scooped up some of his supplies from the counter without looking the proprietor in the eye. He walked out feeling a mixture of shame and defeat. He hardly noticed the footsteps behind him.

'Let me help you with them supplies, friend.'

'I don't need no help. Thanks just the same.'

'Ah, come on. Ever' man needs a helpin' hand now and ag'in.'

Andy turned to see a man who had a smile that was friendly and reassuring, as if there were no problem he couldn't solve. The face belonged to a stranger. But then, Andy's so-called friends had been avoiding him of late, probably afraid he'd ask them for money.

Nolan returned the stranger's smile with a fragile grin. 'Well, I'd be obliged if you'd get those two bags of oats I left on the counter. That'd save me a trip back.' It would also save him the embarrassment of having to face Carl Womack again but Andy didn't mention that unpleasant truth.

'Sure. That your wagon across the street?'

'Yep.'

As they loaded the wagon, the men exchanged names. Nolan noticed that Ricky Cates's clothes were new and not cheap.

When the work was finished, Cates's smile was still strong. 'Let me buy you a beer, Andy.'

'No, thanks. I gotta get back to the farm. There's a long day ahead.'

The smile turned sympathetic. 'From what I was hearin' back in the store, all your days are gettin' pretty long, Andy.'

'Sure are...'

'Come on. Let's enjoy a mug. I have a little plan that will let you pay all of your debts and walk the streets of town with your head held high.'

Andy stopped pacing about the barn, and whispered a curse to the floor. How could he have been so damned stupid? While the two men sat at a corner table in the saloon, Andy had blabbed everything about himself and his farm to Ricky Cates. And yep, Ricky Cates had a plan to help him get out of debt.

At first Andy had been stunned by Cates's offer. 'I ain't no hold-up man. All I can do is scratch dirt and right now I ain't doin' too good at that.'

'Most of my gang are jus' like you, Andy. Honest, hardworking men who need a little help. I give 'em that help. I don't work with crooks but with honest, poor folks who jus' need a helpin' hand. And the job will be easy. After it's over, we'll divy up the loot and you can go back to bein' an honest farmer. Only you'll be

36

a farmer with some money in his pocket. A lot of money, to be factual.'

'I don't know … '

Cates gave his companion a gentle pat on the back. 'I like you, Andy. You're an honest man. The kind who believes in playing by the rules. That's the way it should be.' Ricky took a sip of his beer before continuing. 'But those rules don't always work. No, there comes a time when a man's gotta break a few rules in order to survive in this world. I know you care a lot for that pretty little wife you've been tellin' me 'bout. You wanna give her a fine life. Well, to do that, you're gonna hafta break a few rules … just for one day. Otherwise, you'll lose that farm of yours and then what will you do?'

Andy Nolan began to walk about the barn once again. Ricky Cates was a good talker, he had to give him that. The man had actually convinced him there was nothing wrong in holding up a stage-coach. Hell, it was just one of those pesky little things you had to do to get along in life, like putting up with bad weather.

Andy Nolan whispered a curse once again and stopped his pacing. He didn't want Priscilla to know her husband was a thief. But he couldn't lie to her anymore. That would do no good. He would confess to his wife, then take the money into town and accept the consequences for what he had done.

Nolan closed his eyes and looked upward. He mumbled a mix of words which made no sense. He intended it as a prayer and hoped the Lord could straighten it out. He stood paralyzed, realizing that a hanging could be in his future. Maybe they would be burying the shotgun in town in just a few hours. He hoped not.

'No sense in waiting any longer. I gotta tell Pris the truth,' he said to the roof and all that was above it. 'Gotta do it now.'

Andy Nolan opened the barn door only to be stopped by a high-pitched squeal. 'Pris!' His wife lay on the ground, gagged, with her arms tied behind her.

Nolan didn't know where the assault came from. A sharp pain spiralled inside his head and he suddenly collided with the ground. As he struggled to get back on to his feet, a gun appeared only inches from his face.

'Good mornin', Andy.'

'Ricky ... Ricky Cates.'

'That's right. Git up, you worthless sack of garbage.'

Nolan had barely made it on to his feet when Cates grabbed the front of his shirt. 'Take me to the money, Andy. Right now. Or I'll kill that pretty little woman of yours.'

Nolan sputtered to his glowering captor, 'We agreed ... '

Cates shook the young rancher. 'Don't do no talkin'! You see, I'm in a right ornery mood. That stupid Allan got himself caught and killed by two detectives. The dogs who tried to stop the robbery. So now, those dogs are sniffing on my trail. Just be nice, hand over your $300 and I'll make you a promise.'

'What's that?'

'After I'm finished with your woman, I'll send her back. Otherwise — '

Andy turned a frightened look toward

39

his wife. 'Did — '

'Not yet. You see, I believe in business before pleasure. Get the money, Andy!'

5

Dehner awoke just as dawn was initiating its attack on the darkness of night. Sam Wilcock had already started a fire. The older detective was on his feet, sipping coffee from a tin cup.

'Help yourself.' Wilcock gestured toward the coffee pot on the spider web that bannered over the flames.

'Thanks, Sam.'

'I'm not hungry, what about you?'

Dehner understood the intent of the question. 'My stomach's fine, coffee should be enough.' Rance got to his feet and looked around as he indulged in a morning stretch. 'I see you've saddled Allan's horse.'

Wilcock shrugged his shoulders as if the matter was of little importance. 'Not a bad saddle, if the ... if the family we're taking it to doesn't need no extra saddle they'll be able to sell it. A few extra dollars can always come in handy.'

Wilcock couldn't remember the name of the family who would be receiving the horse. Still, Dehner realized how important this act of kindness was to Sam Wilcock.

Dehner also reflected on Sam's lonely, isolated life. Over a year ago, a family had invited Wilcock to have dinner with them. For an hour or so, Sam had felt a part of that family. He may not remember the family's name but he still remembered where their home was located and still cherished the memory of that day.

Rance poured himself a cup of java. 'I'll drink this while I saddle up. We need to get going.'

By the time both detectives had their horses saddled and broke camp, the sky was providing adequate light for tracking. Dehner and Wilcock both examined the tracks that were on the other side of the knoll from where they had camped for the night.

'Cates is riding pretty hard,' Dehner looked down at the ground from his horse.

Wilcock had dismounted and was crouched over the tracks. 'Yep, he's riding off to meet with one of his buddies.'

'What do you mean?'

Wilcock looked in the direction of where the tracks were headed. 'When a gang divides the money, everyone is on guard in case somebody decides to draw his gun, kill the others and take it all.'

Rance understood what his colleague was saying. 'But once they break up, the crooks relax. They become an easier target.'

'They're easy targets all right, Cates sees to that.'

'I don't follow you, Sam.'

Sam Wilcock sprang up and walked over to his horse. 'Way I see it, Cates likes to work with amateurs. From what you said, Jamie Everett was no hardcase.' Wilcock pointed a thumb backwards where a grave had been dug the previous evening. 'And that kid was pretty green. Cates works with fools.'

Dehner smiled in a sad, whimsical

manner. 'A fool and his money are soon parted.'

Sam mounted his sorrel, which had a rope tied to the horn of its saddle. That rope connected to the reins of Allan's horse. 'Ricky Cates makes damn sure that old saw comes true.'

The detectives began to ride at a steady gait, following the trail of the outlaw. Wilcock suddenly gave a loud laugh. 'Talk about an amateur. One of the crooks was fool enough to tell Cates where he lives.'

'How do you figure?'

'Cates isn't heading back to the stream to pick up the trail. He knows where his man is going.' Sam looked ahead in silence for a few moments before continuing. 'We should turn up ahead to ... to leave the horse, won't take long.'

Dehner noticed a new edginess in Wilcock's demeanour. 'Sure.'

Wilcock still seemed edgy.

Fifteen minutes later, the two detectives approached a small ranch that the word 'hardscrabble' would still describe. But

44

everything about the place shouted of more prosperous times to come. The corral looked well cared for. The barn appeared sturdy and plenty large. It was built for better days that lay ahead.

Wilcock had told Dehner that the couple who owned the ranch had one kid. The ranch house was also built for the future and a large family. A line of cactus plants ran across the front of the house divided by a large porch. Dehner had never thought of cactus plants as being attractive but he had to admit that the plants gave the house a charming look.

The man who stepped out the front door and on to the porch promptly destroyed all effects of charm. He was a large-boned man with muscles that came from hard work and dealing with hard men. His face reflected suspicion as he watched the two detectives approach.

'Mornin', gents.' The rancher's greeting was abrupt and held no welcome.

'Morning,' Wilcock gave the rancher a two-fingered salute. 'Remember me?'

The large man's voice remained abrupt. 'No.'

'Name's Sam Wilcock, I'm a detective. A year or so back, I stopped here while I was trailing some owl hoot ... '

'I remember you now.' The suspicion in the rancher's eyes diminished but only by a fraction.

The door of the ranch house opened and a woman stepped out. She was trying to appear casual but it was obvious to Dehner that she had been listening from inside. A boy of about five was beside her and she had an arm draped around his shoulder.

'Good morning, Mr Wilcock.' She forced a smile in Wilcock's direction. 'In case you forgot, my name is Irma. My husband is Roger.' She squeezed her boy's shoulder. 'And this here is Roger Jr.' She laughed awkwardly. 'Oh and our last name is Travis. This ranch is the Tall T.'

Irma was a heavy set woman, slightly on the short side with black hair and hands blotched by red. Her forced smile became more quizzical as Wilcock introduced Dehner but her voice remained polite. 'Nice to meet you, Mr Dehner. We're jus' finishing up breakfast, you gents are sure welcome to join us.'

'Thanks but no, we ain't got the time,' Wilcock replied.

'Then whatcha here for?' Roger asked.

Wilcock's sorrel snorted and tossed its head as if it had picked up on the tension in the air. Sam pointed nervously at the riderless horse behind him. 'Rance and me got an extra horse, thought maybe you folks could make good use of it. It's a fine animal.'

Roger Travis took a step forward, in what appeared to be an act of aggression. 'Look, Mr Detective, maybe I only got a small ranch here with not much more than ten head, but I don't need no charity.'

Rance Dehner held up a palm, trying to calm the situation. 'It's not charity at all, Mr Travis, but we can't use the animal and Sam remembered you folks. Sam figured that when it comes to running a ranch, an extra horse can always help.'

Irma's eyes bounced momentarily toward her husband, who was still angry. Her forced smile still held as she returned her eyes to Sam Wilcock. 'Where did the horse come from?'

'A dead outlaw,' Sam answered. 'We buried him a ways back.'

'Did you kill him?' Roger Jr. spoke for the first time.

Sam paused for a moment as if he had to think over the question. 'No ... no, I didn't ... he was killed by his partner, a man named Ricky Cates, we're after Cates now.'

'Have you ever killed anyone?' the little boy persisted.

Wilcock stared into space as he responded. 'Yes.'

'How many?'

'That's quite enough, young man.' Irma's firm words were directed to her son but the anger that shoved the smile off her face was aimed at the detectives. These two oafs were ruining her family's morning and all because of one horse. She didn't try to keep the irritation out

48

of her voice. 'Please excuse Roger Junior, we're obliged to you for the animal — '

Sam Wilcock's face went red. He began to shout at the Travis family. 'I don't jus' kill, there's more to it than that. A lot more! I help people! You can ask Rance, I've gotten back money that belongs to honest people. People like you and — '

From inside the house came the sound of a baby crying.

Rance spoke in a low voice. 'Sam, it's time we were going.'

'Yes.' Irma tightened her hold on her son's shoulders. 'The baby needs me. I want to thank you gents for the horse. Please come by when you're in this area again. We'd love to repay your kindness with a good meal.'

Irma had fulfilled the dictates of propriety. She gave her husband a long stare. A silent communication passed between them. Irma hurried into the house, still tightly embracing her little boy.

'Like my woman said, we're obliged for the nag.' The rancher's stern voice conveyed no gratitude as he stepped off the porch and approached the horse that had belonged to Allan.

Dehner watched his partner carefully. Wilcock's face was pale and resigned. Sam Wilcock hadn't understood exactly what he was looking for when he came to this small ranch, but he knew now he wasn't going to find it. Without speaking, he untied the rope on the horn of his saddle, which held the reins of the extra horse and handed it to Travis.

The baby stopped crying. Irma could be heard singing an off key lullaby.

Wilcock turned his sorrel and began to ride off. Dehner rode beside him but didn't speak until they were at a safe distance from the Tall T Ranch.

'Well ... that's done, Sam. We can get back to trailing Ricky Cates. Get back to our job.'

The last few words of Dehner's remark seemed to spark Wilcock. 'Yes ... yes, we've got a job to do. That's the most important thing.'

6

Both detectives focused on trailing Ricky Cates and said nothing about the encounter with the Travis family. Less than an hour away from the Tall T, the two detectives were riding on a bluff. Sam held up a hand for them to halt.

'Something's going on in that field down below. Put your glasses on it, Rance.'

Dehner grabbed his field glasses from one of his saddle-bags. 'Two men and a woman. The woman seems to be wearing a nightdress. One of the men has a gun. They're walking toward those trees.'

Wilcock's voice was laced with suppressed excitement. 'Does it look like our boys?'

'Could be,' Rance replied. 'The jasper with the gun is tall and wiry ... looks like Cates. The other is average size ... hard to tell if he was one of the other hold-up men.'

'How 'bout the trees they're heading for?'

'From what I can tell the trees are spaced reasonably far apart, but the further you go into the woods the thicker it gets ... oh no ... '

'What happened?'

'The woman fell down. The gunman pulled her up by the hair and slapped her.'

'Whatever's going on, we need to stop it!'

They rode their horses down to flatland, then dismounted and began to tie their steeds to a nearby tree.

'Cates is a dangerous man,' Sam Wilcock said in a low voice. 'And our first concern is those people he's holding prisoner.'

'Right,' Dehner replied quickly.

'But if we can, we'll take Cates alive.'

Dehner nodded his head and smiled at his friend. The real Sam Wilcock was back.

Both detectives checked their guns as they turned and ran toward the trees and the three specks in the distance.

7

Ricky Cates looked at the carvings on the tree. ' 'AN LUVS PN'.' Well now, ain't that sweet? Of course, what's buried here is even sweeter. Start diggin', Andy.'

Nolan looked angrily at Cates as he positioned the large shovel. 'I want you to promise me you'll leave us be once — '

'That weren't part of what I tole you.' Cates looked at Priscilla Nolan, standing to his right: barefoot, wearing a night-dress, hands tied behind her back, and gagged. 'I'm gonna take your woman with me. But when I'm done with her, I'll turn her loose. That is, if I got the money.'

To emphasize his point, Cates raised the six shooter in his right hand. 'Now, you get to diggin'!'

'OK.' Nolan started to dig. Priscilla Nolan began to cry. Mournful noises made their way through her gag.

Cates turned his head to her. 'Shut

up.' When he turned back, Andy swung the shovel, trying to hit the outlaw in the head. Cates ducked, took a step toward his adversary, and smashed his gun into Andy's face. Nolan spun backwards, but managed to stay on his feet.

'I didn't kill you, because I want you to dig that hole.' Cates waved the gun at Nolan, his eyes flaming with hatred. 'But don't try it again!'

From behind him, Cates heard the sound of scrambling feet. He turned in time to see Priscilla Nolan tumble to the ground. The woman had tried to run off but stumbled.

The gunman quickly turned back around to face Andy. 'Put that shovel down.'

'How do you expect me — '

'Put it down!'

Andy dropped the shovel. Cates took a few steps toward Priscilla, who was now on her knees as she struggled to stand up with her hands tied.

'There's been a change of plans.' Ricky Cates lifted his gun and pointed it at the woman. 'Too bad, little darlin'. We coulda had some fun, but you're jus' too much trouble.'

'Drop the gun, now!' Sam Wilcock burst out from one of the trees. Rance Dehner was behind him.

Cates pivoted toward Wilcock. The detective and the outlaw fired at the same time. Ricky Cates felt the wind from the bullet that winged inches from his head. The outlaw's shot found its target. Sam Wilcock staggered backwards and collided with Dehner. Both men went down together in a tangle.

Andy Nolan grabbed the shovel and slammed it into Cates's right shoulder. A sharp pain ignited in the outlaw's arm and he dropped his gun. Cates then ducked a second attack from Nolan as he spotted Dehner getting to his feet. The odds were now against him and Nolan was scooping up the gun he had dropped. Ricky Cates ran.

Rance crouched over his wounded comrade. 'Take it easy, Sam. We'll get you to a doctor — '

Wilcock's eyes were glassy. 'Go after that guy, Rance. I'm OK.'

Dehner tried to sound cheerful and encouraging. 'We'll catch up with that owl hoot. For the second time in two days, he was able to slip away because other folks were concerned about helping someone who was hurt. That jasper sure does take advantage of people's good nature.'

Sam Wilcock couldn't pick up on Rance's artificial humour. A greyness descended over his face, and his voice was becoming faint.

'I gave that snake a chance to surrender. That's the way ... should be ... tell the people ... those people who laughed at me ... '

Andy Nolan had untied his wife's hands and removed the gag from her mouth. The woman was a bit unsteady but as she knelt down beside Sam Wilcock, the gratitude on her face was shining forth.

'I don't know your name, sir, but you saved my life. I'm powerful grateful.' After a pause, she added softly, 'Always will be.'

The woman's face was pale and tear streaked, but she still managed something close to a smile. That was the final thing Sam Wilcock saw on this side of eternity.

Rance Dehner tightened the bags on the saddle of his bay. Andy and Priscilla Nolan watched him nervously. They were standing in a grassy clearing near a fresh grave.

'Why don't you stay the night, Mr Dehner?' Priscilla asked. 'It's already mid-afternoon, I could fix us all a fine meal and ... '

'No, thanks,' Dehner replied, 'I need to be moving on. I appreciate you allowing me to bury Sam Wilcock on your land.'

'The least we can do!' Priscilla spoke loudly. 'And I'll take good care of that grave, Mr Dehner. Put fresh flowers on it whenever I can.'

'That would be very nice, Mrs Nolan. I don't think Sam had much of a woman's touch in his life.'

No one spoke for a moment or two. Andy Nolan looked at Dehner

57

apologetically. 'Appreciate what you're doing for me. Hope this don't land you in no trouble.'

'No trouble,' Dehner said abruptly. 'You've returned the Wells Fargo money you stole. One of your fellow thieves is dead. I'll say one crook gave us the slip. No big deal, Wells Fargo will be interested in capturing or killing Ricky Cates and retrieving the rest of the money.'

'I sure am sorry for what I did, Mr Dehner, but the bank kept giving me so much grief — '

Dehner had heard enough. He took a step toward Andy and there must have been something threatening in Dehner's eyes, because Andy Nolan inhaled as if bracing for an attack.

'Stop whimpering, Nolan! Do you think you're the only rancher who ever had problems with a bank? It happens to loads of people, but they don't become outlaws.'

The detective stood motionless and looked at the ranch house and barn in the distance. Still farther on, he could see the wooded area where Sam Wilcock had died. Dehner let out a deep sigh and then faced Nolan again.

'You stupid fool, you almost got your wife killed and yourself hung. What happened here ... ' Rance paused. 'If the shotgun had been killed, I'd have taken you in. I should do it right now!'

Both Andy and Priscilla looked terrified. Rance shook his head to indicate they had nothing to be afraid of. When he spoke again his voice was lower. 'You're getting a second chance, Andy. A lot of men don't. This time, do right.'

'I will, Mr Dehner.'

Rance nodded his head. While mounting his horse, he looked at Priscilla while touching two fingers to his hat. As he rode off he heard Priscilla shouting, 'God bless you, Mr Dehner' but he didn't look back. His mind was on finding the man who had killed Sam Wilcock.

8

Deputy Rollie Owens stepped into the sheriff's office and gave his boss a crooked smile. 'I was right, Sheriff! That dangerous gunslinger Glenn Sampson was yellin' 'bout was nothin' more'n a saddle tramp. No need for you to go runnin' ever' time that restaurant owner squeals 'cause some bug's flown into his ear.'

Sheriff Tom Laughton returned the smile but still looked nervous and apprehensive. 'Thanks, Rollie, but I still think I should have — '

'You shoulda nothin'!' Rollie walked over to the gun rack on the left side of the office's one desk and placed his Henry in it. 'Sampson's a good enough man but he's nervous as a cat in a bell tower.'

Tom moved away from the window where he had been looking out, to the pot-bellied stove on the office's right side.

'Guess I'm pretty fidgety myself.'

'You jus' ain't got much experience. After a year or so, you'll be able to handle townspeople as well as you handle outlaws.'

'Hope so.' Tom poured a cup of coffee from a pot that sat on the stove. He was tall, with black hair and an aquiline profile. He carried about 170 pounds. As a child, Tom's playmates had razzed him about his big nose. About the time he was eleven and experienced a growth spurt, the razzing stopped. At twenty, no one made jokes about Tom's nose; at least not in earshot of the sheriff.

The deputy approached the stove. His boss handed him the cup of coffee and then began to pour one for himself. 'Things are all wrong here, Rollie. You should be sheriff and I should be your deputy.'

'Bull!' Rollie took a sip of coffee, as he casually glanced around the office. 'I ain't got the tempermint to be sheriff. I'd git the whole town mad at me in no time.' He barked out a laugh. 'You'd hafta protect me from the good citizens of Cooper, Arizona, who'd wanna string up their sheriff.'

Tom laughed good-naturedly and, not for the first time, made a silent, off-hand attempt to guess his deputy's age. Rollie Owens could have been anywhere between forty-five and sixty. He was a short, overweight man with a horseshoe of grey hair around his bald head. Tom was the third sheriff Rollie had served under and had a reputation for being no man to fool with.

'Rollie, you have taught me a lot during my four months or so on this job. I sure appreciate it.'

Owens stared into his coffee. 'I ain't taught you a thing you wouldn't have learned by yourself.'

Laughton realized he had embarrassed his deputy with the compliment and needed to change the subject. 'Tell me about the saddle tramp.'

'I got him to pay for his food. That put Sampson in a better mood. The tramp tole me he was lookin' for work as a ranch hand. So, I tole him to get out to a ranch and get started. He left town and the way I see it he won't be back. The fella didn't impress me as a man who cared much for workin' steady.'

Both lawmen were guffawing over Rollie's story when the office door banged open and a nine-year-old boy came running in.

'Sheriff, Mr Rollie, they told me to come git ya!'

'What is it, Bud?'

'Stagecoach jus' pulled in. It's been robbed! The shotgun took a bullet!'

As the sheriff and his deputy arrived in front of the stage depot, a large crowd had gathered. Lou was being helped on to a stretcher by the doctor and two townsmen. Charlie gave Tom and Rollie the details of the hold-up.

'Sounds like them detectives were worse than useless,' Rollie said.

'Never mind none of that!' Charlie snapped. 'The stage's been held up and Lou's been shot. Whatta you lawdogs intend to do about it?'

Charlie's question was followed by angry shouts from the crowd. Tom Laughton could understand the outrage. Lou had lived in Cooper, Arizona all his life and was well-liked.

'Rollie, I want you to get up a posse,' Laughton said. 'Meet me in about fifteen minutes in front of the office. I'm going to check with Carl Womack. I'll get him to look after things while we're gone.'

Loud voices again boomed from the crowd as men volunteered for the posse and vowed revenge on the stagecoach robbers. No one noticed the man who quietly disconnected from the boisterous activity and ambled off, following after the sheriff.

9

Tom charged into Womack's General Store. Carl Womack was behind the counter opening a crate of canned peaches.

'Howdy, Sheriff. I've been hearing a lot of ruckus. Anything wrong?'

Tom gave him a quick report on the stagecoach robbery. Carl listened intently. Neither man paid any attention to the newcomer who strolled into the store and began to casually examine the goods on the shelves.

' ... so Carl, I'll need you to serve as acting sheriff while Rollie and I are gone.'

'How long do you reckon that'll be?'

'A week at most. If we haven't caught any of them by then, we might as well give it up.'

Carl shrugged his stooped shoulders. Tom Laughton didn't catch the nervous undertone in the store keeper's voice.

'Hell, Sheriff, that gang has likely broken up by now and gone their separate ways.'

'Yep. But I'm hoping we can capture at least one. Maybe he'll tell us something about the rest.'

'Maybe, and at least you'll recover some of the loot.' Carl fiddled with his beard. 'You know, Wells Fargo has a lot of pull in these parts … '

The lawman nodded his head. 'I know.' The sheriff was a man of reasonable ambitions. If he could come to the attention of Wells Fargo for helping capture the robbers of one of their stagecoaches and retrieving at least some of the stolen money … well, something good might come of it.

Carl reached across the counter and gave Laughton a friendly slap on the shoulder. 'Sure, Tom, I'll be pleased to do my part and sorta keep an eye on the town. Get the word out that if there's any problems, folks can come and get this old soldier.'

'Thanks, Carl, appreciate it.'

Tom Laughton hurried out of the store.

He had told Rollie he would meet up with him and the posse in fifteen minutes. He was already a couple of minutes behind. As he hurried down the boardwalk, he hoped Carl Womack would make a decent acting sheriff. He should work out all right. After all, Carl had a heap of military experience.

The sheriff arrived in front of his office where a posse of seven men, including Rollie, were already on their horses. Ten more people, eight women and two elderly men, were standing on the board-walk shouting words of encouragement and caution to the men.

'Carl Womack is acting sheriff,' Tom shouted to the people on the boardwalk. 'Be obliged if you'd all spread the word.'

'We will, Sheriff! You bring back those outlaws!' came one shout. Another voice added, 'Dead or alive!'

Laughton mounted his piebald and led the posse as they rode out of town. Rollie Owens rode by his side. The deputy felt very uneasy. Carl Womack had served in the army. But Womack was also a

67

blowhard and Owens doubted the truth of his heroic tales. Rollie believed his boss should have picked a different acting sheriff but didn't want to embarrass him in front of the townspeople.

We ain't gonna be gone for long, Rollie thought, nothin' to really worry 'bout. Still, the deputy couldn't vanquish his sense of dread.

Carl Womack smiled at the slightly familiar man that approached the counter. 'Hello, neighbour, anything I can get for you?'

The large man with a craggy face caught the edginess in the store owner's friendly greeting. Duke Bodine's appearance could make people nervous. The outlaw figured that was good in a way, not so good in others. People remembered a man who unnerved them. 'Got myself a sweet tooth today.' He pointed to a wide jar on the counter. 'Like a scoop of that candy.'

'Sure.' Womack grabbed a scoop and a small bag off the shelf behind him and began to fill the customer's order.

'Sounds like there's been some excitement in town.'

'Yep.' Womack relaxed; the customer seemed friendly enough. He quickly summarized the details of what the sheriff had told him. Details Bodine had already listened in on. 'I sure hope Lou is going to be OK.'

'I would go with the posse,' Duke lied, 'But I jus' took on out at the Lazy L. Old man Jackson wants me there at noon tommorra.' Duke Bodine had heard a ranch hand, standing near him at a bar, complain about old man Jackson, the owner of the Lazy L. Bodine had never actually been near the ranch.

'Mr Jackson has his ways of doing things,' came the bland reply. Carl Womack didn't want to say anything negative about one of his best customers. He made a fold at the top of the bag and set it on the counter.' That will be ... is everything OK?'

Bodine pretended to be scratching his forehead. In truth, he was holding a hand over his left eye which was blurry. What he saw with his good eye didn't please him.

Carl Womack watched with trepidation as his strange customer whispered curses and moved away from the counter.

10

Duke Bodine was still muttering curses the next day as he sat near a pile of grey embers.

He had camped out the previous night a few miles outside of Cooper. The job ahead demanded that he spend some time in town but he wanted to keep out of sight as much as possible.

The sun provided plenty of light and Bodine held one hand over his left eye as he read the dime novel which he had spotted the previous day in Womack's General Store. The novel was titled *Ricky Cates: The Robin Hood of the Range*.

The story ran for thirty-seven pages and Duke read it quickly. He checked the back cover to see where the dime novel had been published. 'New York. Figures. I wonder how Cates met up with a fool writer from the East.'

Bodine looked at the front cover and,

this time, cursed loudly. 'Why did that idiot Cates let someone draw a picture of him to get put on a book cover?'

The outlaw tossed the book aside and got up to warm the coffee. Pain shot through his right thigh. He limped to the fire. As he stoked the embers, a few modest flames erupted and the outlaw began to pace about, trying to walk off the agony that now seemed to throb through most of his right leg.

Duke Bodine was fifty-two and felt every minute of it. The problem with his leg had started a few years back as a minor irritation but now was causing him to occasionally bawl like a bratty kid.

As the pain eased, Bodine stopped pacing and removed a tobacco pouch and papers from his shirt pocket. Why had he joined up with Ricky Cates, a man who was obviously sick in the head?

The answer was simple enough. He had met Cates a few weeks back in a saloon. The outlaw gave a caustic laugh. Throughout his life he had met most of his business partners in a saloon.

Cates had wanted him in on a stage-coach hold-up. One of his gang had been caught pulling a solo job and Cates needed a replacement. 'Most of my guys are young and strong but greener than grass on a fresh grave. I could use an experienced gun.'

Duke closed one eye as he laid a thick line of tobacco across the brown paper. The hold-up was to take place near Cooper. For almost a year, Bodine had been planning something big in Cooper. A stagecoach robbery would fit in perfectly.

Everything seemed to be lining up just fine: a green sheriff, an experienced deputy who was now out of town, a soft storekeeper serving as acting sheriff ... everything except Ricky Cates.

Duke returned the makings to his shirt pocket, lit his smoke and slowly inhaled. He hadn't dropped anything while building his smoke. That was becoming increasingly unusual.

Bodine watched the smoke from his cigarette dissipate into nothingness. His days of being an outlaw were coming to an end and he knew it. Soon, he'd be limping all the time, would maybe need a crutch. And the sight in his left eye had been getting more and more blurry since a bullet winged his noggin. He could still see the outlines of things from his left eye, but it was going out on him.

He still looked tough. His hard, threatening glare had backed opponents down from fights they probably would have won. How much longer could that last?

This job had to work. The money was big. He could disappear into Mexico and live the rest of his life in comfort ...

Duke slapped a hand over his bad eye as he heard approaching hoof beats. It was Ricky Cates. Bodine was expecting his accomplice but as he lowered his right hand, he kept it close to his gun.

Cates dismounted, tied up his pinto to a tree branch, and walked quickly towards Bodine. 'Hello, Duke, see you got some coffee ready. Mind if I — '

'Help yourself.'

'Like for me to pour you a cup?'

'Not right now.' Bodine needed his left

hand to smoke and he wanted to keep his right hand free. 'Well, Ricky, did you get the money from those pups you had working with us on the hold-up?'

For a moment, Cates's eyes remained on the java he was pouring into a tin cup. Those eyes gradually moved to Bodine. Ricky Cates stepped away from the fire and glowered at his companion. 'Don't know what you're jawin' about, Duke.'

Bodine gave his companion a mocking laugh. 'That's a new Smith & Wesson you're toting, Ricky. Maybe one of the pups had a sharper bite than you expected.'

'Maybe we better get to talkin' business, Duke. This here is supposed to be a business meetin'. You tole me you had a really big job in mind and that the stagecoach robbery would help out.'

'You jus' made our business deal a little harder, Robin Hood.'

'Whattaya mean?'

As Cates asked the question, Bodine stepped back, grabbed the dime novel off the ground and handed it to him. The expression on Ricky's face was that of wonderment, like a small boy beholding his first Christmas tree.

'Where'd you git this?' Cates asked.

'At Womack's General Store in town. The storekeeper tole me that book is a right popular item. He's almost sold out. Jus' got two copies left.'

Ricky looked anxiously toward his horse. 'I gotta get me one of those.'

Bodine grabbed his companion's right arm. 'You fool! You can't walk into the store and buy a book with a drawing of you on the cover! Womack or somebody would figger out you're ... '

'But — '

'You can keep my copy of the damn thing. I've read it.'

'Thank you!' That was the first exclamation of gratitude anyone had heard from Ricky Cates for a long time. 'That writer who talked to me did the drawing too, I never guessed he'd put it on the front of a book, I'm going to be — '

'The book cover could end up on a

wanted poster. Maybe you should shave that Buffalo Bill beard of yours and let a barber take some scissors to the long hair. Then you wouldn't look so much like the guy on the cover.'

'Yep. Reckon I'll do that soon.'

Bodine laughed inwardly. Cates was lying. The man was so proud of his good looks, he'd never change a thing. Hell, Cates wanted the world to know who he was — the Robin Hood of the Range. Duke reminded himself that he had one more job to pull with this idiot. Then he'd get as far away from him as he could.

Duke puffed on his cigarette while Ricky Cates sat down and read the dime novel. Cates would occasionally let out a loud yelp, cheering on his fictional counterpart as he took from the rich and gave to the poor.

'I'm gonna be famous!' Cates shouted after he finished the book. 'Why, they'll probably write songs 'bout me.'

Bodine shot a stream of cigarette smoke toward Cates as if it were an act of war. 'Think we can talk business now?

I'm sure you want more riches to hand over to the poor folks.'

'Give me a minute.' Ricky sprang up and carried the book to his pinto, where he carefully placed the treasure in one of his saddle-bags. For the outlaw, leaving a copy of *Ricky Cates: The Robin Hood of the Range* lying on the ground would amount to an act of sacrilege.

Cates strutted back toward his companion. 'Now, tell me 'bout this big job you've got lined up, Duke.'

While Cates was reading the dime novel, Bodine had finished his smoke and built another one. Ricky Cates made him very nervous. 'Last year at this time I was in Cooper, lying low between jobs. Heard some barflies jawing about Russ Adams.'

'Russ Adams. Heard of him. He's the president of the bank in Cooper, ain't he?'

'Yep. And he keeps the place as safe as a fort, most of the time.'

A harsh look of glee filled Ricky's face. 'Most of the time?'

'Every year during this month, Adams has to make up reports of some kind for the government.' Bodine waved his left hand as he spoke, scattering ashes from the cigarette. 'He works late every night. Alone. His wife brings his supper to him around seven.'

Cates was beginning to take a strong interest in the conversation. 'You heard talk last year. Are you sure that's what's happenin' this year?'

Bodine nodded his head. 'I hung around Cooper last night and kept my eyes open. Shirley Adams brings her husband food packed in a picnic basket. She walks around to the back door of the bank and knocks twice. She then waits and knocks twice again. Her husband lets her in. She stays there with him for about an hour. They probably eat together.'

Ricky Cates barked out a laugh. 'And you think we should join them for supper!'

'A road runs behind the bank. More of a path, really. Woods are on the other side of the path. We hide behind some trees. When Adams opens the back door of the bank, we run out of the woods, grab his wife and force our way in. You hold a gun on Mrs Adams while I threaten Russ Adams: empty out the safe or his wife takes a bullet.'

The expression on Cates's face was gleeful. 'And all this happens while the sheriff, his deputy, and a posse are out tryin' to hunt down a gang of stagecoach robbers.'

'And the acting sheriff is a joke.' Duke related what he had heard in Womack's General Store the previous day. 'The great army hero didn't even make one round last night.'

'Maybe we should keep an eye out tonight. Make sure that actin' sheriff don't make no rounds and the little wifey brings her husband the grub.'

Bodine shook his head. 'No. We need to act fast.'

'Why? From what you tole me, the sheriff plans on keepin' the posse goin' for 'bout a week.'

'Funny thing about posses.' Bodine's voice indicated no amusement. 'A posse is always a group of outraged citizens out to get the bad men. But the outrage don't seem to last long. No, a night or two of sleeping on hard ground, far away from family, good food and the work that makes 'em money and a posse's outrage just bleeds out like a pig with its throat cut.'

'Guess you're right. They could be back by tomorrow. That green sheriff is leadin' a posse that's likely to never find the stage-coach robbers.' Cates stopped speaking. He was about to reveal that he knew one of their cohorts was dead and the other had returned to the life of a farmer. That would amount to a confession that Bodine was right. He had been trying to take money from his fellow thieves.

If Duke Bodine caught the slip of tongue he gave no indication of it. 'We make our move tonight,' he said.

Cates nodded his head in agreement. 'Guess I still got plenty of time.'

'Time for what?'

'Why, to read 'bout myself again.' Cates turned and headed for his pinto and the saddle-bag where *Ricky Cates: The Robin Hood of the Range* was safely tucked away.

11

There was less than a half moon in the sky when Bodine and Cates stood silently together in the woods behind the bank. Only a few stars were scattered about against the black canopy and both men figured luck was on their side. The night was reasonably dark. Even if their plans went a bit loco and someone spotted them, they wouldn't be able to see much.

Nearby their horses nickered. Duke tensed up. If the banker's wife heard those nags while bringing her husband's supper she might become suspicious. Why would horses be tied up behind the bank? The lady wouldn't have to think long to answer that question. Anger flashed through Bodine. How could he have made such a stupid blunder?

No time to make any changes, Shirley Adams appeared from the wide alley that separated the bank from a gun shop. She carried a picnic basket. The horses didn't whinny but Bodine still felt uneasy. Ricky Cates gave a long appreciative sigh at the sight of Mrs Adams.

Bodine's distrust of Ricky Cates ignited into hatred. The man was a total fool. Yes, Shirley Adams was a beautiful woman, though a dozen years or so older than Cates. Couldn't the crazy guy put his feelings in check long enough to pull a bank hold-up?

Bodine realized again that 'crazy' was the word for Ricky Cates and thought himself loco for teaming up with him. Too late for turning back. Shirley Adams was now knocking on the back door of the bank for the second time.

As the door opened, both men yanked their bandannas up to their noses and ran toward it. Russ Adams saw them coming. He grabbed his wife's right arm and jerked her inside with one hand while starting to slam the door with the other. Bodine threw his body against the almost closed door and forced his way in.

Adams delivered a hard punch to the

middle of Bodine's face. The outlaw yelled in pain, drew his gun and pointed it at the banker. 'Stop right there or I'll kill you and your wife.'

Several dishes and cups smashed against the walls and floor, sounding like muffled gunshots. Shirley Adams had used the picnic basket as a weapon. Through a haze caused by the punch he had absorbed and his bad eye, Duke could see Ricky Cates force his arms around the woman and pin her back to his chest as he champed a hand over her mouth.

'Now, just take it easy, darlin'. No reason you and I can't be friends.' Cates seemed to be enjoying himself.

Duke Bodine wasn't enjoying himself one bit. He knew Russ Adams was young for a bank president, probably not much past thirty-five but he hadn't reckoned on Adams's strength and aggressiveness.

'You hurt my wife and I'll kill you!' Adams yelled at Cates.

'Calm down and nobody will get hurt.' As he demanded calm, Bodine realized

his own hands were shaking. He was beginning to sense that his good luck had
run out. He was feeling woozy. Blood
dripped from his nose. It might be broken. Someone outside may have heard
the breaking dishes or his yelp.

Duke inhaled. He had to stay calm and
move fast. He looked about. They were
all in a narrow hallway. A few feet down
the hall stood an open door, which must
have led to Russ Adams's office.

'Where do you keep the safe?' Bodine
demanded.

'In there.' Adams pointed toward his
office.

'Open it, and be quick.'

'Don't, Russ, don't...' Shirley Adams's
voice was muffled but still strong.

'Now, you jus' let your husband and my
friend tend to business, darlin'. You and I
should be concentratin' on pleasure.'

Cates's implied threat to his wife
moved the bank president to action.
'Come on.'

The office was large as was the safe
inside it. Russ crouched in front of the

black object and began to work the combination. That act rattled Duke Bodine. Duke hadn't been able to crouch like that for years. The bank president was more nimble than the man who was holding him up. Bodine was becoming increasingly edgy. Some of the blood leaking from his nose soaked his bandanna while the rest of it dropped to the floor.

As the door to the safe opened, Bodine yanked a flour sack from where it had been folded up in his back pocket and tossed it to the bank president. 'Put the money in there, all of it!'

Russ Adams began to comply with the request. As he did, Bodine could hear a low feminine voice purring from the hallway. 'You certainly have strong arms, Mr Outlaw.'

'Maybe these strong arms should hold you a little tighter, darlin'.'

'You need to be a little more trusting, Mr Outlaw. A woman can't very well show her appreciation to a strong man who's holding her so tight that she can't even turn around...'

Shirley Adams was trying to con Ricky Cates. Bodine tensed up even more. Cates was just crazy enough to...

'There!' The banker, still in a crouch, handed the bag back to Bodine. Duke began to feel better as he grabbed the loot. Maybe this scheme would work after all.

His good feelings didn't last. Running footsteps sounded from the hall along with the sharp creak of a door being frantically pushed open. Shirley Adams's voice screamed for help. She was screaming from outside.

Ricky Cates could be heard bellowing a string of curses, which were followed by a gun firing twice and a woman's cries. Duke briefly swerved his head in the direction of the noise. When he looked back, Russ Adams was on his knees with a pistol he had removed from the safe. Both men fired at the same time and both men hit their targets.

Duke twirled and then got off a second shot which hit Adams as he was folding up and collapsing. Bodine staggered from the room into the hallway; he felt weak and he holstered his gun in order to hold the flour sack and the treasure it contained with both hands.

Bodine made it outside. He walked about aimlessly, almost tripping over the dead body of Shirley Adams. He heard hoof beats and saw Ricky Cates ride up on his pinto. In his weakened state, Duke didn't give a thought to the fact that Cates hadn't brought along another horse.

Ricky hastily dismounted, walked over to his companion and took the flour sack from him. He peered inside then gave his companion a broad smile. 'Mighty thoughtful of you to bring this to me, Duke. But, say, you look a mite tired, best you lay down a spell.'

Cates drew his Smith & Wesson and fired a shot into Bodine's chest. Duke Bodine went down, once again cursing himself for getting involved with a lunatic. Through blurred vision he saw Cates ride off.

He started to yell profanities at his

partner but it all came out as a tinny, anguished laugh.

12

Carl Womack tried to sound casual as he raised his voice. He wanted to drown out the sounds coming from not far up the street. 'The damage will be one dollar and ten cents, Wess. Hope I'm not taking your last penny!'

Wess Pickford barely smiled at the store owner's joke. The medium-sized man with skin tanned from long days in the sun reached slowly into the pocket under his bib overalls and looked out the door of Womack's General Store. 'Did ya hear them gunshots?'

Womack gave a loud, theatrical laugh. 'Probably just a few ranch hands blowing off steam at the Lucky Penny or the Red Horse saloons.'

'You're actin' sheriff. Shouldn't ya look into it?' Wess dropped a dollar and a dime on to the counter.

Carl scooped up the money. 'No

need for me to play nurse maid to some barflies.'

'When did ya do your last round?'

'I don't have time to walk around town. I've got real work to do!'

Pickford's face reflected anger at the store owner's gruff reply but he said nothing. He shot Womack a hostile smirk, then walked out with his bag of canned goods.

Carl Womack wanted to call out to Wess and apologize to him but he couldn't do it. An apology would have to end in him admitting Wess had a point and he should take a look to see who was firing those shots.

Womack's body began to tremble. Why had he agreed to be acting sheriff? The answer to that question was easy enough. After telling all those tales of his heroism as a soldier, he really had no choice.

'You damn fool,' Womack whispered to himself. The only danger he had seen in the army came from a typhoid epidemic that swept through the fort where he had been stationed. He had not gotten sick, a fact unlikely to impress people.

Impressing others was important to Carl Womack, so he had made up yarns of bravery and daring do.

The store owner inhaled deeply and tried to calm himself. Those shots probably were the harmless work of a barfly. No need to worry. Sheriff Laughton should be back with the posse in another day or two. Nothing much would...

Bud Lewis came running into the store. 'Mr Womack, you gotta come quick!'

Bud lived with his grandmother but spent most of his time wandering around Cooper, looking for things to do. Carl gave the boy occasional chores, and paid him in candy. While Bud would be sweeping the floor or stacking shelves, Carl would enthrall him with tales of fighting hostile Indians.

The store owner nervously grabbed a bag and scoop from behind him and walked toward the jars of candy on the counter. 'Now, what's so doggone important that it could keep a boy from some delicious treats?'

Bud was stunned by Carl Womack's

reaction. Mr Womack had given him candy before but always in exchange for doing a job. Besides, much as he loved candy, this was no time for it. Now was a time for action!

'Mr Krammer, the mayor, tole me to come getcha! The bank's been robbed!'

Carl Womack stood in silence, looking down at the bag and scoop as if he had forgotten their purpose. Bud heightened the volume of his voice. 'The mayor says you need to come quick. I think Mr Adams has been shot. His wife too, maybe!'

Confusion and suspicion began to cloud Bud's eyes. Those eyes looked far different than when they were full of hero worship as Bud listened to Womack's army stories.

'Well … guess I'd better get over there.' Womack tried to keep a tremor out of his voice. He put down the items in his hand, walked around the counter and was at the door of the store when he realized he was wearing an apron. He began to untie the white cloth.

'Guess ya cain't go after killers wearing one of them things.' A gaze of hero worship was beginning to return to Bud's face.

'Guess not.' Carl walked back to the counter, gently placing the apron on it.

'Aren't ya gonna take a gun with ya, Mr Womack?'

Carl Womack owned an old Sharps which he kept under the counter of his store. It had laid there for years. Carl wasn't even sure if it was loaded. But keeping his heroic image for Bud was important to him. The store owner made a fist and winked at the lad. 'I won't be needing a gun.'

A smile of admiration spread across Bud's face, like sunshine engulfing a stray pup. 'We best get goin'.'

As they hurried up the boardwalk toward the bank, Carl once again began to tremble. He got nervous at memorial services where there was an open coffin. How could he...

A crowd had gathered outside the bank. People parted for the acting sheriff all too quickly. Bud followed behind his

94

hero, but was stopped by a female hand that grabbed the boy's shoulder. 'You stay here, Bud. Inside is no place for you.'

'Ah, I wanna — '

'You heard me!'

'Yes, ma'am.'

Carl was relieved to have the boy taken care of, but still very tense. As he entered the bank, the place stood empty of people. A door leading to a hallway was open and a weak yellow light emanated from the dark hall.

As Womack approached the hallway, he could hear a low murmur of voices but couldn't make out their words. He entered the hall and walked toward a lighted office.

Inside the office, Dr Fred Blaine was on one of his knees beside a body Womack immediately recognized as Russ Adams, though he quickly moved his eyes away from the corpse that had been one of the town's leading citizens. Seth Krammer was crouching on the other side of the body. Krammer was a saloon owner and Cooper's mayor.

Dr Blaine let out a long sigh and ran a hand through his thick brown hair. 'He's gone, Seth. I'm sorry.'

'You did your best, Fred. It's a miracle he lasted this long, taking two bullets at close range.'

Both men got up slowly. The doctor removed the stethoscope that had been around his neck, picked up a black bag from the floor and placed the instrument in it. Seth turned and noticed Carl for the first time.

The mayor nodded a greeting. Both his face and voice were grim as he pointed at the open, empty safe. 'You've got a tough job ahead, Carl. The sheriff and Rollie took most of the town's best men when they went after the stagecoach robbers. But you'll need to ride after the bank robber. This town can't survive without that money.'

Dr Blaine also nodded at Carl. 'I'm going to contact the undertaker. There's nothing more I can do here.'

Seth thanked Blaine. After the doctor had departed, he turned his attention to

Carl. 'I'll ride with you. We should leave at daybreak. I don't think we'll have any trouble picking up the trail of the robber.' He looked at the empty safe. 'I guess we can take comfort in knowing that there is still some way old warriors can make themselves useful.'

'We're ... going after a killer?'

Seth Krammer misunderstood the question. 'Yes, I'm sure this is a two man job. One of the crooks is now dead. His body is lying outside along with that of Shirley Adams. I'll show you.'

As the mayor stepped by him, Carl realized that Seth Krammer really was an old warrior. Seth had served in the War Between the States. Krammer was now a man in his mid-fifties with white-grey hair and a thick white-grey moustache. But he was in fine condition and could usually tame any outbreaks at his saloon, the Lucky Penny, without calling in the law.

As he followed him down the hallway, Womack realized that the mayor never talked about his combat experiences. No one in town would have known about his heroism if an old comrade of his hadn't passed through Cooper a couple of years back. Bud Lewis should be looking up to Seth Krammer and not to a liar like himself. Carl Womack experienced a sensation of shame for the false stories he had told.

Krammer stepped very carefully out the back door of the bank. He turned around to his companion and pointed at the corpse of Duke Bodine. 'This was one of the hold-up men. He was still alive when I got to him, said his name was Duke Bodine. He told me he was shot down by his accomplice, Ricky Cates. I've heard of Cates. He's a very dangerous man, a cold-blooded killer.'

Womack nodded his head and tried to look strong, while not looking too long at the dead body.

The saloon owner continued to speak. 'Like I told you, Duke isn't the only dead body out here.' He nodded toward his left. 'It seems Cates was holding Shirley Adams hostage. She escaped. He went after her and ... well ... I've seen some terrible things in my life, Carl, and I know you have, too. But never to a woman. I just wasn't expecting this.' Krammer motioned for Womack to follow him as he stepped toward the corpse of Shirley Adams. 'The first bullet entered her head and —'

Carl Womack let out a loud scream and began to run. He stumbled over a stone in the narrow road and fell face down. He began to sob uncontrollably, his hands clawing at the dirt as if he were trying to dig a hole to hide in.

Krammer hurried over to his companion and crouched beside him. 'Carl, what is it?'

'It's not true, none of it is true ... '

'I know how you feel, Carl, none of us want to believe — '

Womack continued to look at the ground. He couldn't face Krammer. 'I mean it's not true ... all those stories about my army days ... they were lies ... I never even saw one bit of action ... I can't go after a killer, Seth, I just can't.

I'm scared.'

'Then why did you agree to be acting sheriff? You should have ... ' Krammer stopped speaking. He needed to calm his anger. Seth felt both contempt and pity for the man lying in the dirt in front of him. But the saloon keeper knew how dangerous people could be when they were scared. There were now a lot of scared people in Cooper, people who had just had their life savings snatched from the bank. Many of them would be looking for a scapegoat.

'Go back to your store, Carl. Right now. Forget about being acting sheriff.'

Carl Womack slowly lifted himself to his feet but continued to stare at the ground. His beard was covered with dust and wet from tears and drippings from his nose. 'I can't go back to the store. The people out front will see me like this.'

Seth gestured toward Womack's General Store. 'This road takes you right to the back of the store. Is the back door locked?'

Carl Womack pressed his lips together

and nodded his head.

'Do you have the key with you?'

'I think so.' He reached into a side pocket and brought out a key.

'Good for you!' Seth spoke as he would to a small child. 'Go inside your store and lock yourself in. Don't open up for anyone, except me.'

Womack nodded his head vigorously as he got up on his feet and moved quickly but cautiously down the dirt road to his store. A wave of angry shouts surged from the main street and Womack responded by elevating himself on to tiptoes.

Seth Krammer sighed and tried to keep his contempt for the store keeper in check. Carl Womack was a decent enough man, guilty only of being a braggart and a liar. Those were harmless enough sins ... most of the time.

Womack vanished into the darkness. The saloon owner glanced in the direction of Shirley Adams's corpse, then looked away and began to cry. Russ and Shirley Adams were ... or had been two of the town's finest citizens. The type of people a town like Cooper desperately needed. They were honest and upright people who believed in helping their neighbours and helping the town to grow. On several occasions when he had become discouraged as the town's mayor, Russ and Shirley had...

Another explosion of angry voices ripped the night. Seth Krammer stopped crying. He wasn't Carl Womack. Someone had to maintain order in a town now in the throes of fear, mourning and hate. A dangerous combination, especially when no one knew where to direct that hate.

Krammer marched quickly through the bank and out on to the boardwalk. The crowd there was growing bigger. There were a few women but the gathering consisted mostly of men, many of them with alcohol on their breath. Seth smiled inwardly, noting the irony. Many of the men had received the energy that sparked their outrage through alcohol purchased at his saloon.

'Where's Carl Womack?' Thorny Johnson shouted. Thorny stood at medium height with a thick scraggly salt and pepper moustache. He was a prospector who did much of his prospecting at the Lucky Penny. 'We wanna know what he's gonna do about this!'

'Carl isn't the acting sheriff anymore,' Krammer replied in a calm voice, 'I am.'

'Says who?' Thorny demanded to know.

'I say so.' Krammer's voice remained calm but became more forceful. 'I'm the mayor of this town, I can appoint myself acting sheriff.'

Irma Wieland, the owner of the town's one dress shop, spoke up. She was a large-boned woman with a booming voice. 'Mr Mayor, what happened to Carl Womack? I saw him arrive here, he looked OK to me.'

'Carl isn't feeling well, I ... don't know exactly what the problem is,' Seth Krammer lied.

'I know what's wrong with him!' Wess Pickford's voice was loud and angry. 'I was in his store when all the trouble broke out. I heard the shots. I asked him if he was gonna look into it, him bein' the actin' sheriff and all. You know what he tole me?'

'No, Wess, what'd he say?' Thorny Johnson smelled trouble and liked it.

'He tole me he had too much important work to do in that store of his, to find out what the shots was all about.' That statement got Wess the attention of everyone in the crowd. Wess Pickford was a man people usually paid little heed to. He wanted to prolong his moment in the sun. 'Then he said he had never done a round since bein' made actin' sheriff. Tole me it was beneath him what with him bein' an important store owner. Let me tell you, he spoke high and mighty like.'

'Womack takes the money for bein' actin' sheriff and then he lets the town go to hell!' Thorny Johnson yelled.

'The position of acting sheriff doesn't pay anything,' Mayor Krammer lifted his voice to be heard over the crowd which was noisily declaring agreement with Thorny. 'Carl Womack was a volunteer. He was just trying to do his duty as ... '

Irma Wieland spoke at the same time the mayor did. Her voice was clear and loud, though she was speaking primarily to herself. 'Carl is just a blowhard. Our young sheriff didn't realize that. Now, two of our town's finest citizens have been murdered. And the money we worked so hard for is gone.'

The resigned tone of Irma's voice caused Seth Krammer to fall silent. He liked and respected Irma, who was a widow with her life savings in the bank. He felt genuinely sorry for her but wished she hadn't spoken up when she had. Irma had inadvertently provided the trouble makers with more ammunition.

Thorny Johnson grabbed that ammunition. 'Since Carl ain't feelin' so good, I think maybes we should pay him a visit. Maybe clean up his store for him.'

Wess Pickford realized he was still at the centre of the action. People were actually listening to what he had to say. He picked up on the threatening tone of Thorny Johnson's last remark.

'Since we ain't got money no more, 'cause of Carl Womack, I say we all go over to his store and take what we need right off the shelves. I don't want to give any more of my hard earned money to the uppity no good who thinks he's better than the rest of us!'

Many in the crowd began to shout in agreement as Dr Blaine stepped on to the boardwalk accompanied by the undertaker, a middle-aged man with deep set eyes. Both newcomers were carrying a crudely made stretcher. The crowd made the undertaker edgy and the doctor motioned for him to go inside the bank.

Dr Blaine was holding the stretcher by himself as he whispered to the mayor, 'As soon as I'm finished here, I'll give you some help, if you need it.'

Seth nodded his head in appreciation. 'Thanks, Fred, looks like I'm going to be needing all the help I can get.'

13

As Rance Dehner rode into the town of Cooper, he patted his bay gently on the neck and spoke in a whisper. 'I'm going to spend some time in a watering hole and see if I can find out anything about Ricky Cates. He may have been through here, for that matter, he might still be here. I'll get you to a livery, in an hour or so.'

Dehner smiled whimsically at his own words. He reckoned he wasn't the only man who, spending long hours away from human company, found himself talking to his horse.

Angry shouts from down the street shattered the detective's whimsical mood. He spurred his horse to a fast walk. Dehner was surprised to see an angry mob gathered in front of the boardwalk that fronted Womack's General Store.

Angry men shouting for revenge was

nothing new to Rance. But these dangerous gatherings could usually be found in front of a sheriff's office, where a crowd was demanding justice by a lynching, or maybe a saloon where one group of beered up cowboys was calling another group to come out and fight.

'What could be going on in front of a general store?' Dehner's words were again spoken to his horse.

The detective saw two men standing in front of the store's entrance. He recognized one man as the doctor who had attended to the wounded shotgun at the stagecoach hold-up. The other man was older but more muscular. His white hair turned iron grey in spots and Dehner suspected that hair colour wasn't the man's only iron-like quality.

Both men were holding Winchesters, though the rifles were aimed downward. The doctor was speaking, shouting really, at the mob of about twenty-five men. 'I've just given Carl some medicine. He's resting now. All of you go home and — '

A loud voice boomed from the crowd.

'Tommorra, Womack will be done restin'. He'll be chargin' us money for stuff we need. He'll be demandin' money we ain't got because he let Russ and Shirley get shot down while he was playin' Mr High and Mighty.'

The crowd began to surge forward. The doctor, to everyone's surprise including his own, fired a shot over their heads. The mob stopped short of the boardwalk. They looked stunned.

But not all of them; Dehner spotted one man break away from the crowd and take a peek down the alley between the general store and a barber shop. The man nodded his head quickly as if he had just received a signal of some kind. He ran down the alley, obviously planning to … well … planning to what?

Rance Dehner hadn't a clue as to what was going on but he had a natural distrust of mobs. And whoever was vanishing into the darkness seemed to be up to no good. The detective tied up his horse at the hitch rail in front of the barber shop and proceeded quietly after the man who was responding to a silent signal.

Midway down the alley, he could hear suppressed guffaws and the alcohol laced voices of men who thought they were whispering.

'Where'd you find the kerosene?' Thorny asked.

'Hotel,' Wess replied. 'They keep an extra bottle under the cou'ter.'

'Did the desk clerk give ya trouble?'

'The desk clerk is out front givin' the mayor and Doc Blaine trouble!'

Both men guffawed. Thorny, still laughing said, 'Toss that stuff all over the damn place. We'll smoke Womack out.'

Dehner had heard enough. He hastily moved to the back of the store. 'Freeze! Both of you!'

'Who are you?' Wess's voice sounded indignant.

'A man who thinks it's hot enough. We don't need any fires,' Dehner replied. His .45 was still holstered. He saw that the two men were standing close together. One had a gun strapped around his waist. The other man was unarmed, dressed in overalls and holding a bottle, no doubt the kerosene.

The detective stepped close to the two men and addressed the one in overalls. 'Give me that bottle.'

Thorny felt that a stranger was robbing him and his friend of their big moment. He couldn't let Wess surrender the bottle. 'I'll give ya what — '

Thorny went for his gun. Dehner landed a fist on the side of his head. Thorny collided with Wess and both men collapsed in a tangle of arms and legs. Dehner first grabbed Thorny's gun which was still in its holster. He then picked up the bottle; it hadn't broken and the cork remained on the opening.

'On your feet, both of you!' Dehner pointed Thorny's gun at the two would-be arsonists. The men got up slowly and clumsily, both of them sputtering curses.

'We're going around to the front.' Dehner motioned with his gun hand for both men to move.

14

Seth Krammer's nervousness increased. The crowd in front of the store was getting increasingly hostile. The mayor realized he was part of the problem. He had told Dr Blaine the truth about Carl Womack. Fred had given the store owner laudanum to prevent a total breakdown.

But Krammer had not told any of this to the crowd. He hadn't exactly lied but he had held back on the truth and they sensed it.

Krammer feared that the truth would make the crowd even more dangerous. Womack was a liar who agreed to be acting sheriff in order to back up his falsehoods. If the mob (many of whom had just had their life savings taken from the bank) knew that, they would become blood thirsty.

Of course, they were plenty blood thirsty now.

'We've done enough yakkin', Seth!' The loud bellow came from Ralph Pine, the town's barber. 'We all got families to feed and no money to do it with because of Carl Womack. Let's break into the store, take what we need and maybe break Womack, too!'

Shouts of agreement exploded across the crowd. Seth pointed his Winchester toward the mob and wondered if he could fire on people who had never broken a law before in their lives. He glanced beside him and realized Fred Blaine was wondering the same thing.

Ralph Pine stepped belligerently on to the boardwalk. Three other men immediately followed and the entire mob seemed to lurch forward. Seth spotted a stranger, holding a gun on Thorny and Wess. The two men who had set off the trouble were now looking sheepish as they emerged from the alley beside the store.

'Hello there, stranger! I see you are escorting two of our town's finest citizens.' Everyone turned to see who Seth Krammer was yelling at, buying the mayor a few more precious moments.

Dehner didn't know exactly what was going on but understood the dangerous threats of violence that festered only a few feet away from him. He kept his voice light and humorous, matching the mood of the man who had called out to him. 'These two gents thought the general store would make great kindling for a camp fire.' The detective held up the bottle of kerosene. 'One of them stole this from the hotel; they were going to splash kerosene against the back of the store and turn it into an inferno.'

Seth Krammer faced Ralph Pine, who now only stood a couple of feet in front of him.

'There's the sort of men you're allowing to jerk you around like a dog on a leash,' Krammer shouted his words; he was speaking to the entire crowd. 'Two worthless jaspers who would start a fire. There is a sharp breeze blowing tonight. How long would it have taken those flames to reach your barber shop, Ralph?' Krammer's eyes darted in a fast glare over the mob. 'That fire would have reached every business in this town before we tossed the first bucket of water on it. By morning, Cooper, Arizona would have been a pile of ashes.'

A hard silence followed Seth's remarks. Most of the mob began to look downward. Ralph Pine and the other men who had joined him stepped off the boardwalk.

Krammer caught the sense of remorse in the men that now stood awkwardly in front of him. He spoke in a forceful but more subdued manner. 'A lot of awful things have happened in this town tonight. Let's not do anything to make it worse.'

The mayor pointed at Dehner's two prisoners. 'I'm tossing those buzzards in jail. Tomorrow morning, we'll take out after Ricky Cates. That's the name of the varmint who robbed the bank. His pard told me that before he died. All of you go home, now!'

The crowd began to disperse. Dehner noted that none of the men looked at each other.

Their shame seemed real but it was

115

temporary. If they had carried out their threats, shame might have possessed them for the rest of their lives, and maybe something a lot worse than shame.

Dehner's voice snapped at his two prisoners. 'We'll just stay here for a moment, the gentleman who just spoke has some plans for you two. We wouldn't want to run off and inconvenience him.'

The detective's eyes briefly shifted to the front of the general store where the doctor was scurrying inside. He was probably checking on his patient. From what Dehner had heard, laudanum could certainly put a man to sleep. But the detective wondered if this Womack fellow could possibly have dozed through the blare of a threatening mob.

The other man who had been blocking the store's front door, quickly stepped off the boardwalk and held out a hand as he approached the detective.

'Thanks, stranger.' The white-haired man nodded toward Dehner's prisoners. 'You stopped these two buzzards from burning down the town and helped me to hold off a scared, crazy bunch of jaspers.' The man's gaze did a quick once-over of the former mob which was now a scattering of men going in different directions, their eyes not meeting. He looked back at Rance. 'My name is Seth Krammer.'

'Rance Dehner.'

Seth smiled broadly at the newcomer. Dehner recognized the smile immediately. It was the smile of a good, proud man who hated to do it but was about to ask for a favour.

Dehner was right.

15

Rance Dehner rode in front of a sullen, angry collection of men that could no longer be called a posse. Deputy Rollie Owens was on the detective's right, riding a strawberry roan. Sheriff Tom Laughton was riding his piebald on the detective's left. Both lawmen looked grim. Understandable. They had found out about the murder of Russ Adams and his wife and the successful bank robbery about a half hour before when Dehner had located their camp.

One of the men riding behind them spurred his horse into a lope and then began to ride alongside the sheriff. He spoke to the young lawman in a strident yell. 'When we get back to town, ya better wire all 'round 'bout the hold-up and killin's.'

A chagrinned look filled Tom's face but he kept his temper in check. 'Thanks,

Elroy, but from what Mr Dehner has told me, Mayor Krammer has already sent out several wires. US Marshals are probably looking for Ricky Cates right now.'

Elroy wasn't going to leave it there. 'Ya know, ya fell fer the oldest trick in the book. Leavin' town to go after stagecoach robbers, you shoulda — '

Deputy Owens had heard enough. 'Elroy, you never read a book in your life and the oldest trick you know is dumping blame on other folks. Now, get back with the others!'

Elroy glowered at the deputy but obeyed his orders. After he had left, Tom spoke softly. 'I got that right, didn't I, Rance?'

'Yes. Seth sent out those wires as soon as he could. He asked me to track you down and bring you back to town. As he sees it, the search for Ricky Cates will take a different turn now.'

'Any turn will be better than this one!' Rollie Owens said. 'I've ridden with a few good posses but damned few. Most posses turn into a bunch of cry-babies like this bunch.'

The now rag tag collection of grumblers rode into town at about mid-morning. Dehner immediately sensed a tense atmosphere. News about the murders and robbery had obviously spread. There was a large contingent of people in front of the sheriff's office. But this crowd was different than the one that had gathered in front of the general store the previous night. There were a large number of women present and no barflies. Dehner reckoned those jaspers were still sleeping it off somewhere.

The detective recognized one of the men standing in front of the sheriff's office: Seth Krammer. Another man stood with Krammer. He was a tall, skinny man with thin black hair that was retreating to the centre of his head.

'Who's that?' Rance pointed at the balding man.

'Reverend Zack Peavy,' the sheriff replied. 'He's the pastor of Cooper's only church. Good man.'

120

Most men from the failed posse rode off in different directions, though a few remained on their horses, watching the drama in front of the sheriff's office from a distance. Dehner and the two lawmen quickly dismounted, tied up their horses and joined the two men on the boardwalk.

Seth Krammer was addressing a lady in the crowd. 'I can't promise when the bank will reopen, Cara. As soon as the money is recovered, we will get back to normal business operations as soon as possible.'

A male voice shouted out from the back of the crowd. 'How can you be so sure the money will be recovered?'

Tom Laughton took on that question. 'Rollie and I just got back. We know what happened and what we have to do. This isn't a job for a posse. This is a job for a few men who won't come back until they have that money. We will get the money back! And the man responsible will be brought to justice!'

A middle-aged man with skin tanned more red than brown spoke in a calm but worried voice. 'But, meanwhiles, how're we gonna live? Most of us had our money in the bank and...'

Seth Krammer nodded his head in a sombre manner. 'I believe Reverend Peavy can best answer that question.'

The pastor took one step forward. He didn't really need to, his voice carried naturally over the crowd. 'My wife, Etta, and I talked with Carl Womack this morning. Carl is still quite ill but he is deeply concerned about the crisis facing our town.'

A voice once again screeched from the back of the crowd. 'Concerned! Hell, all of this is his fault. Carl Womack don't give a damn 'bout no one except hisself.'

Reverend Peavy obviously recognized the shouter and looked directly at him. 'This is not the time for careless accusations, brother! Carl Womack has agreed to extend credit to everyone in this town until the bank reopens. Etta and I will run the store and keep the records. Brother Womack is ill but he still realizes how important it is for the folks of this town, and that means all of us, to stick together!'

The pastor paused as a loud chorus of amens followed his remarks, then continued. 'The service for Russ and Shirley Adams will begin at one this afternoon. I will see you all there. If you have any business to attend to, I suggest you do it now.'

The crowd began to wander off. The five men on the boardwalk hurried into the sheriff's office. Tom spoke immediately to the pastor. 'What's the real story with Carl Womack, Preacher?'

'Carl's nerves are shot!' Reverend Peavy replied. 'He can't face anyone right now. We have to keep him isolated.'

'Was this notion of extending credit really his idea?' the sheriff asked.

Peavy shook his head. 'Etta and I talked him into it. I have no idea how long he will cooperate. We haven't got much time.'

'You're right about that, Preacher,' Krammer said. 'Time is precious. I have an idea to make the most of that time.'

Seth's four companions gave him a curious stare; he continued to speak. 'Dehner, your agency has been hired by Wells Fargo. They want their money back and they want Ricky Cates captured or killed.'

'That's right,' Dehner agreed.

'So, get to it! Tom, I think you should ride with Dehner. Of course, Tom, your job is to retrieve the bank's money.'

The young sheriff looked uncertain. 'But — '

Seth Krammer wasn't uncertain. 'Rollie can look after the town. I'll give him any help he needs.'

'Mayor, I...'

'Tom, Rollie and I know the folks in Cooper. We've lived here for ages, you haven't. We'll keep the lid on. You capture the man who killed Russ and Shirley, and bring back the town's money.'

'He's right,' Rollie quickly added.

Tom Laughton looked at Dehner. 'Guess we'd better get moving.'

'Ah, gentlemen, before you leave, there is something in the book rack of

Womack's General store that you may find of great interest.'

Everyone looked at the pastor with curious expressions. Dehner noted that Reverend Peavy was smiling for the first time since he had seen him.

'We're in a hurry, Preacher,' Tom replied. 'Are you sure — '

'Oh, yes, I'm sure.' The pastor's smile broadened.

16

Ricky Cates rode slowly as he contemplated his strange situation. He was a rich man with enough money to last a lifetime. He was also tired, hungry, and thirsty with a horse that felt pretty much the same way.

Cates knew the area well but he had avoided the streams. The law would check all the watering holes in order to pick up his trail. Still, his canteen was empty and he hadn't eaten since yesterday when he grabbed a bite before he and Duke robbed the bank. He'd have to find water and food soon, along with a safe place to sleep.

The killer suddenly halted his horse and pulled out his telescope. There was a small, hardscrabble farm up ahead. He rode a bit closer and again made use of the telescope. Yes, that was a well in front of the house!

Normally, Cates would have watched the farm closely before approaching it. But thirst drove him on. Besides, he could easily handle anything or anyone connected with this broken down operation.

As he approached from the side, a tall, bony man emerged from the dilapidated house and on to the small porch. He was carrying some wood. A rope was tied around his waist, holding up his patched Levi's. A hammer rested between the rope and his Levi's and white shirt.

Cates noted that the gent was watching him approach with mild curiosity but no fear. A friendly greeting might be just the thing.

'Howdy!' The outlaw smiled and lifted a hand in a slight wave.

'Mornin'.' The reply was relaxed enough.

'The name is Ricky. Ricky Cates.'

'Uriah Burgess.'

'Uriah, my horse and me would sure appreciate some water from that well of yours. I ain't askin' for charity. I can pay you.'

Burgess eyed the newcomer with an intense interest. 'I ain't never charged no one for a drink of water and don't see no reason to start now.' He pointed toward the well. 'Just git down and help yourself.'

Cates noticed Burgess's strong glare and dismounted slowly, keeping an eye on the farmer. At first, he thought Uriah Burgess had a plug of tobacco in his left cheek but he quickly realized that the swelling was permanent. The farmer's lower face tilted left as if his jaw had broken long ago and healed wrong.

Off his horse, Cates continued to smile but his right hand remained close to his gun. Burgess didn't notice. His attention remained riveted on the face of Ricky Cates.

The farmer pointed a finger at that face. 'Say, ain't there a drawin' of you on the front of a book?'

Cates relaxed a bit but his hand remained close to his gun. 'Yep. Sure is.'

Uriah's face exploded into a smile. 'Thought so! I saw the book last Sunday when I visited my brother Simon.'

'Did you read it?'

Uriah shook his head in embarrassment. 'Nah. I can't read none. Tried learnin' a few years back but it didn't take. But don't get me wrong. I hold high any man who can get his face on the front of a book.'

Excitement came into the farmer's voice as he put down the pieces of wood. 'Say, you go ahead and get some water for both you and that pinto. Afterwards, take your horse to the stable out back where he can rest some. I keep oats there. After you finish with the horse, I should have us some food ready.'

'Thank you, Uriah. I'd be honoured to accept your hospitality.' Ricky Cates then headed for the well which was deep. The water tasted good and, after allowing his horse to drink, he filled his canteen, but as he led his horse to the stable, he thought to himself that it looked more like a shed.

Ricky Cates felt superior to Uriah Burgess. Cates felt superior to everyone, which made it easy for him to kill.

Cates took his pinto to the small stable, removed the horse's saddle, gave him a rub down and then fed the animal. As he did so, he considered his predicament. He needed a place to hide out and rest for a few days. Uriah Burgess's farm was not it. Uriah was too simple a man. He would never understand the Robin Hood of the Range. Uriah was the type who tried to be helpful to everyone. If the law stopped by later on, Uriah would gladly give them every little detail he could think of about the stranger who had paid him a visit. Uriah would never lie to the law.

But maybe Uriah's brother Simon would.

The chow Uriah served was, as the farmer himself put it, 'nothin' special'. Cates couldn't tell what the meat was and didn't ask. No doubt it was some critter Uriah had managed to kill. Cates noted that Uriah Burgess was a man carrying a lifetime of injuries. The old man could no longer be picky about what he shot for food.

The potatoes were dry and

undercooked. But the outlaw was a hungry man and gladly gobbled down the vittles as the small dining table, which had uneven legs, shook beneath him.

While he wolfed down the food Uriah served, Ricky Cates plied the farmer for information on his brother. He didn't have to be subtle. Uriah lived alone and enjoyed having company. He remained excited over feeding a guest, a drawing of whom was on the cover of a book.

'That older brother of mine don't allow himself much in the way of extras. But he surely does like them books Womack sells at the general store.'

'Where does your brother live?'

'About two miles northeast of here.'

There was a slight splattering sound and a fluttering of wings. Uriah looked with disgust at a newly deposited white stain on his floor. 'Damn birds! They build nests in the eaves of my roof. Don't mind that so much but there's a hole in that roof. They get inside and ... well ... you seen what they do. I was gettin' ready to fix that hole when you arrived.'

The farmer looked upwards at two birds who perched on a beam that ran across his peaked ceiling. He let loose with several shouts. The birds remained where they were, indifferent to the curses being hurled at them.

'My brother's wife, Elsie, loves birds. She says there's nothin' sweeter than the songs of the birds. Well, I call it screechin'. Them birds just screech all day while I gotta work in the hot sun. There's nothin' sweet about them creatures, nothin' attall.'

'Why don't you let me help you fix that roof?'

'Why ... thanks ... sure you don't mind?' Uriah sounded as happy to have company for another hour or so as he was to have help fixing the roof.

'Happy to lend a hand,' Cates declared. 'It's the least I can do after you fed me all these great vittles.'

'That's sure nice of you. Elsie says birds do good things like eat bugs and worms. Well, they don't eat the bugs that bite me. And what do I care if they eat worms? That don't do me no good.'

After they were done eating, Uriah retrieved a rickety ladder from the stable and placed it against the side of the house. He handed Ricky Cates several pieces of wood. 'I got the nails in my pocket.' Uriah patted the left side of his Levi's. A hammer still rested in his belt. 'You follow me up. I know where the hole is at. We should have this done in a jiffy.'

As Uriah ascended the ladder, Ricky did a fast calculation. The house wasn't as tall as he would like it to be but if he carried out his plan just right, it would work. Ricky Cates was always confident he could do things just right.

Cates didn't bother carrying the wood with him as he followed Uriah Burgess up the ladder. On the roof, he only walked behind Uriah for a few steps before taking out his Smith & Wesson and slamming it against the back of the farmer's head.

The farmer's cry surprised Cates; it sounded like the cry of a small boy being attacked by a swarm of bees. Uriah collapsed on to the roof and Ricky grabbed him before he could slide off.

Cates stumbled and fell. He began to slide downwards but managed to catch his foot on a split shingle. He still had hold of Uriah's right arm. The old man was lying on the roof only a few feet from the outlaw. Uriah's face, now pale and oozing terror, looked toward the sky. Blood from his head took a zigzagging course toward Ricky, who shifted his position slightly to make sure none of it touched his hair or clothes. Cates slowly let go of Burgess. He didn't move. The outlaw cautiously got back on to his feet and walked cat-like to where he could grab Uriah by the ankles.

Uriah Burgess was helpless but not unconscious. He babbled senselessly as Cates picked up his ankles and dragged him to the highest point on the roof. Ricky Cates dangled Burgess head first over the ground below. The farmer screamed in terror as the killer let loose and Uriah dropped to the ground. The farmer's body lay in front of his house.

The act of tossing Uriah Burgess, so

that his body would clear the front porch, caused the outlaw to lose his balance. He fell on to his stomach and once again began to slide down the side of the roof. He managed to drag the toes of his boots against the roof while employing his hands as brakes. He stopped his slide only inches away from the top of the ladder that remained propped against house.

Cates smiled in a confident manner. He had always thought that fate was, somehow, on his side. Stopping right in front of the ladder seemed to confirm the notion.

The outlaw remained confident but cautious as he climbed down the ladder. Uriah's hammer had fallen from his rope-belt as he plunged to the ground. If the farmer had survived the fall that hammer could be used as a weapon.

The killer drew his gun and walked toward the front of the house. Uriah Burgess wasn't moving. The hammer lay at a safe distance from his body.

Cates remained guarded as he approached the body and then crouched over it. 'You got a broken neck, Uriah. Just like I hoped.' The outlaw holstered his gun as he rose to his feet. 'It's not that I didn't appreciate your cookin', Uriah, but you would have told the law that I had been by this way. Can't have that.'

Cates walked briskly to the stable behind Uriah's house and saddled his horse. He left the pinto in the stable as he drew his gun and returned to the front of the house to make sure no one had come by and discovered the body. He then ran back to his steed and mounted it.

Ricky Cates was now more relaxed. He rode his pinto back to the front of the house, where he looked down on the farmer's corpse. 'You know, folks are gonna be laughin' at you, Uriah. Sooner or later some neighbour will find you and say, "That ol' fool had no business to be up there on that roof by himself. Why, he almost deserved to take a tumble.' Yep, Uriah, nobody will suspect that I helped you off that roof. So long, old man, I gotta pay a visit to your brother.'

As he rode off, Cates began to laugh.

He was amused by what was happening all around him.

The birds were singing.

17

'I've been plum foolish,' Tom Laughton declared. 'But not in the way most people think.'

'Nothing foolish about the way you can track a man,' Dehner replied. 'We should be catching up with Ricky Cates ... soon.'

Dehner told the truth about Laughton's tracking abilities but the process was slow and both men were worried. Ricky Cates was a vicious killer who had to know he was being pursued. He wouldn't hesitate to butcher anyone in his attempt to escape capture.

'Most people think the stagecoach hold-up was a trick to get me and Rollie outta town, so the outlaws could rob the bank,' Tom continued. 'I think it's more complicated than that.'

'So do I. Cates seems to be the only link between the two hold-ups. I don't think there was a direct connection.'

Rance was sure Andy Nolan would have told him if the stagecoach hold-up had been part of an elaborate scheme to rob the bank in Cooper. But the detective had let Nolan remain free and couldn't let the sheriff in on that angle. The situation made Dehner nervous.

Tom Laughton was also nervous. 'Folks were right 'bout one thing. I never shoulda appointed Carl Womack acting sheriff.'

'From what I understand, Womack is a solid citizen who does a fine job of running his store,' Dehner said. 'Seth Krammer told me he believed Womack's army stories. Oh, he thought Carl exaggerated some when he told his tales to kids, but Carl is an honest man — in most ways. There was no reason to doubt him.'

'You know, I think Rollie Owens had his doubts about Carl, but kept them to himself. Wish now that I'd asked Rollie for advice on appointing an acting sheriff. I made a bad decision and I'll regret it the rest of my life.'

'Tom, when you are a lawman, you're going to make serious mistakes, mistakes that sometimes cost innocent people their lives. You have to carry those mistakes with you forever. That's the way it works.'

The solemnness in Dehner's voice surprised the sheriff. He was about to ask the detective if he was speaking from personal experience when a cry for help shattered his thoughts. Both men halted their horses.

'Sounded like a child,' Dehner said.

'Came from that direction.' Laughton pointed west. 'There's a ranch over there, the Camerons own it. They have a little girl, she's may be just playing.'

A scream pierced the air, a little girl's voice but this time not conveying any words, only a deep, petrifying terror.

'She's not playing,' Dehner snapped.

Rance and Tom spurred their horses into a fast gallop. The detective rode behind Laughton, the sheriff knew the area better than he did. As the men approached the ranch house, they could hear a woman yelling and a man's voice explode in a primeval screech.

As the two men pulled up in front of the ranch house, they heard the sound of glass shattering. The door to the house stood wide open. Someone had been in too much of a hurry to close it.

Laughton and Dehner slid off their horses. The sheriff drew his gun as the two men ran into the house.

They stood in what must have usually been a pleasant living room. The room was dominated by a sofa and two stuffed chairs. A large throw rug covered most of the wooden floor, or it usually did. The rug was now bunched up and the sofa had been knocked over. A child's rag doll lay beside the fallen piece of furniture. The doll was face up, it's mouth a wavy line of apprehension, as if recovering from an attack.

Muffled sobs emanated from a nearby room. The sheriff and the detective made their way down a short, wide hallway which led to the back of the house and what was obviously a dining room. As they drew closer to the room, they could hear a woman's soft voice.

'There now, everything is going to be all right. The man is gone.'

The sobs stopped, replaced by a shrill, screaming voice. 'It wasn't a man, Mommy, it was a monster!'

When Laughton and Dehner entered the room, both the woman and her daughter were startled into silence. The woman spoke first. 'Tom … Tom Laughton!'

The child spoke up. 'He's the sheriff, Mommy, you know, the sheriff with the big nose.'

'Barbara!'

Both men smiled good-naturedly at the woman's exclamation. Tom Laughton holstered his gun but a feeling of tension hung in the room.

There were quick introductions. Dehner learned that the woman's name was Alice. She and her husband Bill ran a horse ranch. Alice was on her knees beside a dining room table holding her daughter, who appeared to be about four years old. A window on the wall behind the table had been broken. Red curtains with white polka dots now framed a V-shaped shard of glass that had survived the assault. A chair lay outside the window amidst particles of glass which sparkled sunlight in a celebration of the destruction.

'What happened here, Alice?'

Alice Cameron whispered words of comfort to her daughter before answering the sheriff.

'I don't rightly know the whole story. Bill is out with our two hands rounding up horses. I was in the barn when I heard Barbara scream. I came running. When I got inside, I saw Barbara in the dining room. She was terrified and so was I. It was just awful. There was a strange man who held my daughter in his arms — '

'It was a monster, Mommy!'

'OK, honey, OK.' The woman stood up, her arms still holding the child who clung to her. 'The monster seemed to want an apple Barbara was holding. An apple I had given to her before going out to the barn.'

Dehner spoke to the child, who had both arms around her mother's neck but was facing the two newcomers. 'Did the monster want your apple, Barbara?'

The girl nodded her head.

Dehner smiled and spoke in a soft voice. 'Tell us what happened.'

'I was in the living room playing with Annie.'

'Annie is the name of her doll,' Alice whispered.

'The monster grabbed me. He tried to take my apple.'

'Where did the monster come from?' The sheriff also spoke in a gentle voice.

Intensity joined the fear in Barbara's eyes. 'From the woods! Monsters live in the woods!'

Alice gave the two men a chagrinned look. 'I've told Bill not to read her those Grimm's Fairy Tales.'

'Did you hold on to your apple when the monster tried to take it?' Dehner asked the child.

'Yes. He picked me up and kept trying to get the apple. We fell down on the sofa and knocked it over. He got up still holding me and ran here.' She again pointed a finger downward indicating that 'here' was the dining room.

'That is when I came running in,' Alice said. 'I guess I screamed at first, I guess I screamed loud. After that, I told Barbara to give the ... monster ... her apple. Once he got the fruit he put Barbara down.'

'Did he say anything to you?' Laughton asked.

'No,' Alice Cameron quickly replied. 'He looked at me and gave out a cry, sort of like a wounded animal. You know, I think he was hungry, very hungry. He held on to that apple tight with one hand, picked up a chair with the other hand, smashed the window, jumped out and ran away.' The woman sighed deeply as a quiver passed through her body. 'You know, if he had jus' asked I woulda given him food.'

'He must have seen Barbara with the apple,' Dehner said. 'Where do you think he was hiding out?'

Alice Cameron went quiet for a

moment, obviously giving the question some thought. 'You know, Bill told me yesterday that a bag of oats we use for feeding the horses had been ripped open. He thought maybe a stray dog or something had snuck into the barn. But I wonder if maybe it was the monster. Maybe he's been in the woods watching this house. When he saw the men folk leave, he peeked in the window and saw my girl alone with her apple.'

'Makes sense,' the sheriff added.

'I'm glad you two came by, why are you out here anyway?'

Tom Laughton tensed up. He didn't want to scare a woman who had already been frightened enough for one day. But silence could be dangerous. 'Alice, we are trailing after someone who is a lot more dangerous than an apple thief ... '

The lawman gave the lady all of the background on Ricky Cates. While he talked to her, Dehner retrieved the copy of *The Robin Hood of the Range* which he had purchased at Womack's General Store after Reverend Peavy had made him aware of its existence.

When Dehner returned to the dining room, Barbara was no longer in her mother's arms but standing close to her. Dehner handed Alice the book.

She studied the cover carefully. 'No. I haven't seen this man. The apple thief had black hair. He was thin, very thin, and his body seemed almost like it was made out of rubber. His beard was short and scruffy.'

The woman smiled as she handed the dime novel back to Dehner. 'You men are welcome to stay for lunch. Bill and the hands will be back in an hour or so.'

'No, thank you,' Tom said. 'We've got to keep on Cates's trail. And we'll keep an eye out for the apple thief.'

Dehner smiled wistfully. 'Maybe we'll end up catching two monsters.'

18

The Robin Hood of the Range handed three ten dollar bills to an elderly woman. 'That's for you and your husband, Mrs Burgess. Reckon you can use it.'

'Thank you, Mr Cates, but you shouldn't — '

'Sure I should!' Ricky Cates smiled broadly as he spoke. 'Why, you folks have been mighty kind to hide me out these past three days.'

Simon Burgess sat at the dining table in a small house consisting of a dining area, kitchen and bedroom. In front of him lay a copy of *Ricky Cates: The Robin Hood of the Range.*

'This here drawin' of you on the cover is a good likeness, Mr Cates. But won't that be sort of a problem ... '

'Reckon not,' Cates replied. 'Why, every lawdog in the Arizona territory has a description of the Robin Hood of the

Range. I just learn to live with it.'

Elsie Burgess took the three bills Cates had given her and stepped through an open door into the kitchen, where she took down a large jar from a shelf that sided the oven.

'The west certainly needs a man like you, Mr Cates.' She placed the bills in the jar and placed it back on the shelf. 'That banker, Russ Adams, has got plenty of money in his bank. He can spare $200. Folks like us got almost nothin'.'

'That's right, ma'am, and I plan to hand out more of that money, startin' today.'

'Are you leavin' us, Mr Cates?' Simon asked.

'Yes, sir. Been about four days since I robbed the bank. Guess the law has figured I'm far away by now. I need to start handin' out money to poor folks that need it.'

'Well, before you leave, you gotta have a good breakfast,' Elsie declared. 'I'll start gettin' the food on the table. Isaiah should be back from early chores soon.'

Ricky Cates smiled, but he wasn't happy. Isaiah, a hired hand, was a lot stronger than his elderly and frail boss. Cates could tell that Isaiah did not accept the Robin Hood story he had fed that crazy fool from New York. The outlaw hated Isaiah for that. Ricky Cates also hated Isaiah for his black skin.

Hoof beats sounded from outside. Simon awkwardly arose from his chair and hobbled over to the window. He brushed back the thin curtains, moved his head around for a few moments before shouting out, 'It's Pete Tyler!'

'Who?'

'Pete Tyler, a US Marshal, he's got a deputy with him.'

Ricky scooped up the bedroll that lay on the floor. 'Get rid of 'em. Fast!' He rushed inside the couple's bedroom.

Marshal Pete Tyler spotted Simon at the window as he and his deputy, Amos Harrigan, hitched their horses. The marshal smiled and nodded as the two lawmen stepped on to the front porch of the house.

Simon opened the door before Pete could knock. 'Mornin', Marshal, Deputy. Been a spell since you two have been out this way.'

'Reckon so,' the marshal replied. 'Last time we were in these parts was about four months ago, when we were tracking the Sloan gang.'

'Back then, you folks were great about lettin' us put on the feed bag,' Deputy Harrigan's freckled face gleamed with hope. 'We could sure use some of that kindness now. The marshal and me has been ridin' hard. Gettin' mighty tired of eatin' jerky.'

Pete Tyler laughed and shook his head. The marshal stood at medium height, slightly overweight with snow white hair. 'Amos ain't none too subtle. Now, if you folks have already had your breakfast — '

Amos Harrigan's face took on a dreamy look. He smelled the food being prepared in the kitchen. Simon couldn't see any way he could lie about having already eaten. 'No, Elsie and me was jus' getting' ready to sit down. Both of youse are welcome.'

The two lawmen took off their hats as they ambled into the Burgess house. Marshal Tyler felt a bit awkward. It wasn't right imposing like this on folks. If he had been more at ease himself, he might have spotted Elsie's nervousness as she stepped out of the kitchen. After greeting the two lawmen, she fussed with her apron and tried to sound casual.

'What brings you two gents to these parts?'

'Didn't ya hear?' Amos Harrigan spoke loudly as was his custom. 'The bank in Cooper got robbed last Thursday night. We're trackin' the man who done it. An owl hoot by the name of Ricky Cates.'

Elsie's anxiety sounded like anger in her voice. 'Can't see why a US Marshal and his deputy have to make such a big deal over two hunnert dollars. That banker, Russ Adams, thinks he has to have every penny in the territory.'

Marshal Tyler looked confused. 'Ma'am?'

'Well, that's all that got took from the

152

bank. Two hunnert dollars!'

'Where'd you hear that?' A strong curiosity laced Pete Tyler's voice. Cates could hear it from where he stood directly behind the door of the bedroom. The outlaw stared at the six-shooter in his right hand. As always, it gave him a sense of power.

Elsie's nervousness became more apparent. She began to work her hands. 'Why, we heard it in town, yes, why, we was just there yesterday.'

'Who told you that the bank was only robbed of $200?' The marshal was not going to let the matter drop.

Elsie shrugged her shoulders in an overblown matter. 'Cain't recall.'

Tyler's eyes shifted to Simon Burgess. Simon looked at the floor. 'I can't rightly remember who it was myself.'

Pete Tyler's lawman instincts were kicking in. Something was wrong here. Very wrong.

'Well, you've been lied to. The bank was cleaned out of almost ten thousand dollars. And Russ Adams was gunned down in cold blood. So was his wife. Russ was working late and Shirley had brought him something to eat when Ricky Cates and his partner surprised them. Cates killed Shirley while he was robbing the bank. That we know for a fact. Ricky Cates shot down a woman. His partner may have killed Russ, we're not sure.'

Amos Harrigan stopped thinking about his stomach and focused on the strange behaviour of Elsie and Simon. 'Cates also killed his partner, an outlaw named Duke Bodine, so he could have the whole ten thousand to himself. Ricky Cates is a killer who cares about no one 'cept himself.'

'That can't be true!' Simon shouted as he moved beside his wife.

'Why not?' the marshal shouted back. Neither lawman noticed the door behind them opening.

Cates fired two shots: the first ripped into the back of Marshal Tyler, the second plunged through the throat of his deputy. Tyler slammed on to the dining table, his body tipping the table over on its side as the lawman landed on his back.

His deputy dropped to his knees, then went down, splayed out on the floor. Both lawmen instinctively began to reach for their guns as they squirmed on the floor only moments from death. Ricky Cates barged into the room and fired another two shots into the heads of each lawman.

Elsie Burgess began to scream hysterically. 'You ought not, you ought not!' Her husband put an arm around her, trying to calm her, but his body was also trembling.

'Shut up, old woman!' Ricky opened his six-shooter, pushed out the empty cartridges and reloaded from his gun belt.

Elsie continued to scream, 'You ought not, you ...'

Ricky Cates stopped her screams with another shot. The horror of his wife's brutal death was the last thing Simon Burgess saw. Cates sent a bullet into the old man's head.

Ricky cursed himself as he once again reloaded. He should have let Simon Burgess live for another few minutes. He needed to know where Isaiah was. The

Burgesses talked about their hand doing the 'early chores'. What did that mean? Was Isaiah close enough to have heard the shots? Probably, but Cates couldn't be sure.

The killer made his way around the dead bodies, hurried into the kitchen and retrieved the three ten dollar bills from the jar. He again used caution in stepping over the human obstacles as he returned to the bedroom. He didn't want to get blood on his boots.

19

Inside the bedroom, Ricky Cates's bedroll and saddle-bags were lying on a wide bed. Cates returned the thirty dollars to one of the bags containing the money he had stolen from the bank. He had the money from the stagecoach hold-up in a separate bag.

For a few moments, the outlaw gently caressed the two saddle-bags, like an old man touching the heads of his grand-children. All that money made him feel immortal. There was nothing or nobody that could stop Ricky Cates.

His god-like sense of dominance was suddenly destroyed. The outlaw dropped to the floor, using the bed as a shield between himself and the small window in the room. He thought he had seen some movement at the open window. Could Isaiah have been spying on him?

Six-gun in his right hand, Ricky

advanced on his belly toward the window. The outlaw paused to collect himself as he reached the wall, directly under the fluttering curtains. He then sprang up and gazed out the window, ready to gun down any adversary.

There was no one there. Ricky cursed the two birds that were flying about and almost fired at them.

The killer breathed heavily and tried to calm himself. His pinto was out in the barn. He had kept it there purposely. A fine horse tied up in front of the Burgess's place would have attracted some attention. But now he had to reach his steed while keeping clear of Isaiah, wherever he was.

Ricky Cates prided himself on being smart. He paused and thought about everything Elsie and Simon had told him about their hired hand: hard-working, honest, kind …

Cates enjoyed dealing with such men. They were easy to fool. And Isaiah was a black man. The killer's mood became almost playful. This could turn out to be fun. He once again went to his saddle-bags, this time to pull some things out.

Caution was still needed. Bedroll under his left arm and saddle-bags slung over his left shoulder, Ricky Cates left the house and headed for the barn. He tried to look casual but his right arm was free and ready to draw.

'Stop right there, Mr Robin Hood!'

Ricky stopped and turned around. Standing in front of the Burgess house was Isaiah. He was a big man, wearing a chequered shirt and pants made of rugged material. His temples were lined with grey and his arms held an old scattergun.

'Drop everything you're carryin', and take off that fancy gun-belt real careful,' Isaiah ordered. 'You're gonna pay for what you just did. I'm takin' you into town.'

Cates spoke as he carried out the instructions. 'You know, brother, I'm happy you came along. That devil just gets inside me sometimes, and I do horrible things. I hope you can forgive me like Simon Burgess did. He says the Lord will forgive

159

me and so does he.'

A wave of shock passed through Isaiah. 'Mr Burgess is still alive?'

'Sure is.'

Isaiah turned his head toward the house. Ricky Cates pulled a derringer from under his sleeve and fired directly into Isaiah's chest. The killer laughed as his victim went down, collapsing on to the scattergun. 'I use the derringer most times in card games, but it worked just fine on you, Isaiah.'

Cates continued to laugh as he rebuckled his gun-belt, tied down the holster, and gathered up his cargo. Sauntering into the barn, he hummed the tune of a hymn whose lyrics he couldn't remember. As he saddled his pinto, he wondered how long it would be before the dead bodies were discovered. Probably not too long. He needed to be on his way.

But as he rode out of the barn, Cates couldn't resist the urge to inflict more pain. He carefully rode toward Isaiah's body, stopping several yards away. The body of the hired hand was moving a bit.

He was still alive.

'Hey, Isaiah!' Ricky shouted. 'I know you wanna see your good friends Simon and Elsie. Now, bleedin' to death can take a long time.' He drew his Smith & Wesson. 'So, I'll hurry along your journey.'

An explosion sounded from underneath Isaiah's body. Despite his fatal wound, Isaiah had managed to lift the old scattergun and pull the trigger. He had been unable to aim, but his shot didn't completely miss its mark.

Ricky Cates yelled in pain, holstered his gun and spurred his horse. He needed to get away from the Burgess place and find help, find another farm or ranch where the fools believed in the Robin Hood of the Range.

20

'Are you listenin' to me, girl?'

'Yes, Pa.' Cissy Runyan looked down at the food on her plate. She always looked down when her father talked to her.

'Tomorrow afternoon, Harry McGivern is gonna come by. He's lookin' to buy a horse for his boy. The kid's got a birthday comin'.'

'Yes, Pa.'

'I want you to pretty up and be nice to McGivern. Show him that little buckskin we got. McGivern will say the horse looks scrawny. You tell him it will only take a week or so to get more meat on the horse's bones.'

'Pa, if we took better care — '

Dencel Runyan grabbed his daughter's red hair and pulled back. He moved his face in close to hers. Cissy could smell the whiskey on her father's breath. 'You don't tell me how to run the ranch.

Understand, girl?'

'Dencel, please — ' Iola Runyan reached across the table and placed a hand on her husband's shoulder.

'You stay outta this!' The man glared at his wife, who immediately retreated, then looked back at his daughter, tightening his grip on her hair. 'Don't never talk back to me!'

'Yes, Pa.'

Dencel continued to hold on to Cissy's hair.

'Please, Pa, let go. It hurts.'

Dencel Runyan slowly relaxed his grip. He used his free hand to grab a potato from a bowl on the table. As he cut open the spud he glared threateningly at his daughter.

Cissy pushed her food around on the plate for a few minutes and even managed to swallow a couple of bites before speaking to her mother. 'May I please be excused, Ma?'

'Honey, try to eat a bit more. Breakfast is a long way off.'

'The food's very good, Ma, but I just

ain't hungry.'

A look of resignation came over Iola Runyan's face. The woman was accepting one more small defeat. All of her days were becoming a jumble of small defeats.

'I need to get to the barn and tend to the horses,' Cissy spoke in a soft but firm voice.

Iola glanced at her husband who was now shoving food into his mouth, indifferent to the two women at the table. The woman smiled weakly and nodded at her daughter. Iola and Cissy shared a secret about the barn.

Cissy rose from the table, quickly ignited a lantern, and headed outside. She was anxious to get to her escape. The last time the family had gone into town, her ma allowed her to buy a dime novel. Iola had slipped her daughter the money, which Dencel would have wanted to be used toward a jug. Cissy had bought *Ricky Cates: The Robin Hood of the Range* and, so far, had only read it once. The publication now lay beneath a pile of hay in the barn. She was looking forward to a second read.

As she walked past a corral in bad need of repair, the girl wondered if she would ever leave the ranch. At sixteen, Cissy had often thought of running away, but it seemed wrong to leave her ma alone with her pa, who was drinking more and becoming harder to live with by the day.

When Cissy opened the barn door she gasped in surprise and stepped back. She glanced upwards at the sky, where clouds seemed to be playing some strange game with the moon. After a moment, she slowly returned her eyes to the barn.

A magnificent pinto stood inside. Though she had spent her lifetime around horses, Cissy was frightened by the animal. She approached it slowly. The pinto carried a beautiful saddle. Why, this horse looked just like Sherwood, the faithful steed of the Robin Hood of the Range.

Holding the lantern in her left hand, she carefully reached out and began to pat the horse. For a moment, Cissy experienced a moment of magic. Ever since she had turned thirteen, Cissy had done as her father ordered. She had prettied up and helped to sell horses to the men who came to the ranch. Many of the sales had been to men who were looking for a horse as a gift for a son or a daughter, a special birthday or Christmas present.

But there had never been anything special for Cissy. She had long ago even stopped thinking about it. Birthdays came with a quiet, 'Happy birthday, dear,' whispered by her mother. Christmas was a day when her father got even more drunk than usual.

And now ... the girl continued to pat the horse, feeling more comfortable with the animal. This was a real horse, not a creature that somehow popped out of a story. But how...

Cissy heard shuffling sounds nearby. Without hesitation she hurried to the left side of the barn where two lines of hay bales were stacked. She lifted the lantern over the bales and was greeted by the barrel of a gun pointed directly at her.

Cissy gasped again, this time more out

of wonderment than fear. She looked at the man who was lying on the floor.

'You're Ricky Cates!' Her voice was a stage whisper of excitement and adulation. 'You're the Robin Hood of the Range!'

Cates lowered the gun. He knew immediately that the girl wasn't a threat and could be a help. He smiled weakly. 'That's right. I'm him.'

Cissy looked at the bloody mess which was Cates's left shoulder. 'What happened to you, Mr Cates?'

'Ricky. Please call me Ricky. What's your name?'

'Cissy. Cissy Runyan. I live here with my ma and pa.'

Cates broadened his smile. 'OK if I call you Cissy?'

The girl shrugged her shoulders and briefly moved her face out of the lantern light. 'Reckon it'd be all right.' She quickly regained her composure. 'Now, tell me what happened to you, Mr ... Ricky.'

'I robbed a bank of $200. That ain't

167

much money to take from a bank … '

'I've read all about you. You only take a little money from the bank. Just enough to give to poor folks.'

'That's right. And sometimes I depend on poor folks for help. I was holed up at the Burgess place. Know them?'

'Just a little. Our family don't get around much.'

'A posse tracked me there. They opened fire on the Burgess house with no warning at all. Killed Simon, Elsie and that hired hand of theirs, Isaiah. I tried to defend them, but — '

'I know how hard it must have been, what with you only shooting to wound, never to kill.' Cissy moved around the bales of hay and crouched over the gunman, holding the lantern where she could get a good view of the wound. 'It doesn't look too bad. I can pull the buckshot out. Your real problem is losing blood. How long have you been here?'

''Bout thirty minutes.' It occurred to Cates that for once, he was telling the truth. 'After leaving the Burgess place, I stopped by a grove of trees somewhere and tried to make a bandage to stop the bleedin'. Passed out for a while, then got back on my horse. Remember seein' this barn. The door was open. I was half unconscious. Rode in and closed the door. Can't remember much after that.'

'Girl, what's takin' so much fool time?!'

'Who's that?' Cates asked.

'My pa. He ... he drinks some.'

There was another shout. Dencel Runyan was getting closer to the barn.

Cissy looked at the open door. 'Pa will come in. He'll see your horse. He'll start lookin' around and find you.'

Cates started to say something, but the girl hurried toward the front of the barn. She looked near the door. Her hopes were realized: her father had left a jug there that afternoon, as he occasionally did.

Cissy picked up the jug and moved quickly out of the barn. She reached her father as he passed by the corral and handed him the prize. 'Here it is, Pa. Knowed you'd be lookin' for it.'

Dencel had forgotten about the jug but

accepted it gratefully. 'Thanks.'

'A man needs to whet his whistle at the end of the day.'

Dencel was confused. His wife and daughter had never shown much good humour when it came to his drinking. He returned to the question that had brought him out in the first place. 'Whadda you been doin' in the barn?'

'Lookin' after that buckskin. He don't look all that good.'

'What's wrong with him?'

'Don't rightly know. I'm gonna spend the night in the barn. I'll have him lookin' fine by tommorra, Pa. You'll be able to get a good price for him.'

Dencel glanced over his daughter's shoulders. He thought he saw movement inside the barn. One of the nags seemed to be out of its stall. The horse might even have a saddle.

The man's vision began to go fuzzy, as it often did. He uncorked the jug and took a drink.

'First thing in the morning, I'll pretty up, Pa. I'll talk real sweet to Harry

McGivern when he comes to look at the horse. You'll get a lot of money for him. So, all you have to think about is what you're gonna do with the cash. You can start thinkin' 'bout it right now.'

'Maybe I'll do just that.' Dencel turned and began to slowly weave his way back to the house.

Cissy stood and watched her father until he made it inside the house. What would she have done if her lies had failed? The girl didn't know, but she did know this much. She would never have let her pa get past her and find Ricky Cates.

21

Cissy ran back to the barn. She retrieved a bag of clean rags that could be used as bandages, and a few clean tools, including a bucket. The girl stepped outside the barn where there was a pump and filled the bucket about a quarter full. She then hurried over to the outlaw, whose face remained pale.

'This is gonna hurt some, but I'll have you fixed up soon.'

Cates's voice expressed anger and disbelief. 'What do you know about doctorin'?'

A lifetime spent with Dencel Runyan had inured Cissy to harsh words. She accepted the mockery in Ricky's voice as her rightful due. 'I've been brought up on this hardscrabble ranch.' The girl spoke as she undid Cates's makeshift bandage which came from a ripped, dirty blanket. 'My pa likes his drink. All sorts of ugly things happen around here. I don't have much book learnin', but I've still learned a lot. Had to.'

The outlaw became more cautious. He realized, once again, that this girl could help him. His voice became friendly. 'Nobody could accuse you of braggin' on your family.'

'Nothin' much to brag on; my ma is a fine woman, but ...' Cissy held the lantern closer to the wound. 'Not too much buckshot there. You must have been movin' pretty quick.'

The killer caught the strong element of hero worship in the girl's voice. 'There were ... six men in that posse.' He started to say a dozen but realized Cissy lived too close to Cooper and the real world to believe that. 'They were all armed with shotguns or Winchesters. I wounded four of them. Figured they had it comin' for what they did to the Burgesses. Simon, Elsie and Isaiah, why, they were just hard workin', poor people.'

What followed was painful for Ricky Cates, but he remained stoic as the girl removed the buckshot and cleaned the wound. He had to keep the image of the Robin Hood of the Range alive in order to keep himself alive.

Cissy concluded by locating a ladle, putting fresh water in the bucket, and making her patient take several drinks. She held the ladle in one hand and lifted Cates's head with the other. 'You've lost a lot of blood. You're gonna be weak for a spell.'

'Guess so ... thanks for all you've done.'

Cissy allowed the outlaw's head to gently return to the ground. She withdrew her hand slowly, allowing it to caress Cates's cheek. The girl looked confused and upset. She started to speak, then stopped and began again, only this time on a different track. 'I'm gonna give Sherwood a rub down, then put him in a back stall, where he won't be easy to spot.'

The girl used great care in attending to the horse. As Sherwood contentedly chewed on some oats, Cissy picked up

174

the lantern and quietly went back to her patient. Ricky Cates was sleeping but the light woke him up. As his eyes opened, he smiled at the pretty face which hovered over him.

'I'm sorry I woke you,' Cissy said.

'I'm not.'

The girl's body trembled; in her nervousness she forgot about the first name arrangement with her hero. 'Mr Cates, there's somethin' I gotta say to you.'

'Go ahead.'

Cissy placed the lantern down and kneeled beside the outlaw. 'Mr Cates, you've done so much for poor people and you've paid a price for it. I mean, you're sort of like a martyr, like Stephen in the Bible.'

The killer had no idea who Stephen was but he still replied, 'Right kind of you to say that.'

'It's true. That's why, Mr Cates, you must not give us any of that two hundred dollars you took from the bank. Like I sorta told you before, my pa, he's a drunkard. The money you almost died for, my pa would spend on liquor. You give that money to folks that deserve it, Mr Cates!'

'Tell you what, Cissy, I'll give thirty dollars to you! You sure deserve it for fixin' me up.'

'No, I don't want — '

'When Ricky Cates decides to help someone, well, there's just no stoppin' him. I'm givin' you that thirty dollars, Cissy, and only askin' one more favour from you.'

'Yes?'

'I want you to take part of that money and buy yourself a nice dress. A real pretty girl like you should have a pretty dress.'

'I couldn't... ' The girl stopped speaking and looked away. When she looked back, she realized that the light from the lantern made Ricky's face appear to glow like the face of an angel. 'Mr Cates, there is something I want to share with you. Something very special. That is, if you feel up to it ... Maybe I should just leave you alone. You need rest.'

'Nah. I don't want no rest. If you got something special to show me, I know it is special 'cause you're a very special girl.'

Cissy pressed her lips together for a moment. The indecision passed. She picked up the lantern and walked back to the far right corner of the barn. There wasn't much there except hay. At least that is what her father thought.

This small corner contained Cissy's private world, a place where she could escape if only for a few minutes in the day. The girl moved to one area of the hay and pulled out her treasure which she carried back to Ricky Cates.

'Whatcha got there?' Cates asked as the girl carefully arranged her dress and crouched down beside him on her knees.

'Pa don't allow me and Ma to go to church. But, on Sunday mornings, he usually sleeps in late. Ma and me come out here to the barn.' She patted the book that lay in front of her. 'We read from the good book and pray together some.'

The outlaw felt a surge of anger. Over the years, he'd had to put up with a passel of fools who tried to save his soul. But he managed to force a smile.

'That's a mighty decent thing for you and your ma to do.'

Cissy's voice took on a new intensity. 'Something very ... unusual has happened, Mr Cates. I think heaven is speaking to me, speaking to both of us maybe.'

'Whaddya mean?'

'Well, when I read that book about you, I thought about some verses I've read in the Bible ... from an uncommon book.'

'What's uncommon 'bout the Bible?'

The girl missed the killer's unintentional revelation of his ignorance. She continued in an excited voice. 'The verses come from the Song of Solomon. It's sort of an unusual book. A lot of folks don't read it much. It ain't like the four Gospels.'

'But you read it.'

'Yes, and when I read *Ricky Cates: The Robin Hood of the Range*, I realized there's a place in the Song of Solomon that describes you perfectly.' She opened the Bible. 'Can I read you those verses, the ones about you?'

'Sure.'

The young woman inhaled and paused before reading softly. "The voice of my beloved! Behold, he cometh leaping upon the mountains, skipping upon the hills. My beloved is like a roe or a young hart: behold, he standeth behind our wall, he looketh forth at the windows, showing himself through the lattice'.'

Ricky's anger still festered inside him. He didn't know how to respond to words he didn't understand. 'What's a roe?'

'Roe is an old-fashioned word for a deer. A hart is a horse, a boy horse, a stallion.' She pointed at the Bible. 'There is a place in the back where they explain that stuff.'

The killer relaxed. He stopped fighting the fatigue which plagued him and his smile became less forced. 'So, readin' 'bout a horse makes you think 'bout me?'

'It's more than just that, Mr Cates.' Cissy gazed at the roof of the barn as she struggled for the right words. 'Like I said, I thought about this passage when I read the book about you, and it has come true, in a way. You are a man of great strength, who rides a fast horse and like the man in the Bible you have come to my home in a secret like way. It's sort of like ... well ... like God has brought us together. I know how crazy that sounds but I really believe it's true.'

She looked down at the wounded outlaw. Ricky Cates was asleep.

'I'm glad you are sleeping,' she said. 'You need your rest. We can talk about my notions later.'

Picking up the lantern and Bible, Cissy began to quietly walk away. The girl suddenly stopped. For a few minutes, she stood still in the barn. A cacophony of sounds came from outside as night critters made their customary noises, but Cissy Runyan heard none of them.

She turned back and returned to the outlaw. This time, his eyes didn't open when she stood over him. He appeared to be in a deep sleep. Cissy placed the lantern and Bible down as she crouched over Ricky Cates. She didn't really need to open the Bible. She had read this passage so often that it was embedded in her mind. This time her voice was little more than a whisper.

"Many waters cannot quench love, neither can the floods drown it: if a man would give all the substance of his house for love, it would utterly be contemned'.'

She gently kissed the outlaw on the forehead.

'You're the first man I ever kissed, Mr Cates.'

Cissy picked up the lantern and Bible and this time made her way directly to the right hand corner of the barn. She hid the Bible in the usual place, then made for herself a bed of hay. Before extinguishing the light, the young girl took one last long gaze toward the wounded man sleeping in the barn. For the first time in many years, her dreams were happy.

22

Sheriff Tom Laughton studied the ground carefully. 'I'm pretty sure these are Cates's tracks.' The lawman was on foot. The sun was going down and he needed to dismount in order to see the ground really well.

Tom looked at Dehner, who was still on his horse. 'There's a small farm 'round here owned by Simon and Elsie Burgess. If he spots it, I think Cates will stop there.'

'How do you figure?' Dehner asked.

'Ricky Cates may be outsmarting himself. He didn't stop at any watering holes, probably 'cause he knew we'd pick up his trail there.'

'But our killer still needs water,' Dehner said. 'And, for that matter, so does his horse.' Dehner pointed at the ground. 'We know he's been riding hard.'

'Yep, and his stomach must be

hollering. He can't be carrying too much food.' The sheriff sighed deeply and looked around him.

'What's wrong?'

'Simon has a brother, Uriah, who has a place somewhere 'round here. I've never actually been there. I wonder if that's where Cates went when we lost his trail.'

'Could be, Tom. The best thing now is to stop at the farm owned by Simon and Elsie. If nothing else, they can tell us how to get to Uriah's place.'

Laughton put a hand on the horn of his saddle and his foot in one of the stirrups. 'You're right. Besides, we're losing sunlight fast. We're 'bout done trailing Ricky Cates for today.'

As they rode toward the Burgess farm, Dehner noted an unhappy expression on the sheriff's face. Well, the detective thought, there was a lot to be unhappy about.

Dehner tried to lighten the mood. 'Do you think Simon and Elsie might invite us to dinner? A home-cooked meal would taste good.'

'Probably will,' Laughton's reply was toneless. 'Their house is small. No room for two more but they would let us sleep in the barn with Isaiah, the hired hand.'

'Are Simon and Elsie good folks?'

'I suppose so.' Melancholy began to lace Tom's voice. 'Simon's an easy guy to get along with, Elsie is a good cook, but...'

'But?' Dehner prodded.

'Elsie's the type that figures the whole world's out to get her,' Tom continued. 'Everybody's taking what's rightly hers, she never gets appreciated enough, you know the type of person I'm talking about?'

'I sure do.'

'Sometimes, I think Simon should tell his woman to stop complaining all the time.' Laughton's voice was now heavy with sadness. 'Of course, Simon's been married for many years now and me ... I guess I got no place telling another man how to handle women.'

Dehner turned his head and stifled a laugh. He suddenly understood the origin

184

of Sheriff Tom Laughton's unhappiness. 'Is that remark little Barbara made about your nose bothering you a bit?'

Laughton gave his companion a lopsided grin. 'Yep, suppose so.'

'Barbara is only a little girl, not much more than four.'

The sheriff's grin became broader and even more lopsided. 'True enough, but there are a lot of girls much older than four, who look at things the same way Barbara does. I know I'm not a handsome guy but I sure get tired of being reminded of it jus' 'bout every day.'

They rode on in silence for several minutes before Sheriff Laughton suddenly halted. 'This big nose of mine sometimes comes in handy. I smell bad news, Rance. Let's ride a bit slower.'

They hadn't ridden much further when Rance smelled it, too: the wretched odour of death. 'The smell seems to be coming from a distance. That means there has to be more than one body.'

'It could be dead animals.'

'Could be...'

But neither man believed the odour came from anything except human corpses. They continued to ride but only for a few minutes.

'We're only a little ways from the Burgess place,' Tom once again halted his horse. He pointed to his left. 'Let's tie up our nags in that grove of trees and hoof it the rest of the way. I don't want to make any noise going in.'

'Good idea.'

As they proceeded on foot, the smell became stronger and more repulsive. 'The killings must have been done hours ago,' Dehner spoke in a sombre voice. 'The killer is probably long gone.'

'Probably,' Laughton breathed in through his mouth; he seemed to be bracing himself for the horror they were walking toward. 'But let's be careful. Real careful. First thing we get to at the Burgess place will be the stable. We'll stop there and get a look at what's going on.'

Dehner nodded in agreement.

The red sun seemed to be dropping at

an accelerating pace as if it didn't want to spotlight what lay ahead. Laughton and Dehner made their way to the stable. They stood at the back corner and surveyed what lay before them.

Two coyotes were feasting on something that lay on the ground. One of the animals lifted up an object with his mouth: the arm of a man.

'Oh no.' Laughton drew his pistol, intending to run the animals off.

'Wait!' Dehner whispered as he placed a hand on the sheriff's arm. 'I think I see a light moving inside the house.'

Both men stared intently toward the front window of the Burgess home. A pin of light bobbed about, occasionally vanishing.

'There's a window in the bedroom of the house, a very small window,' Laughton also whispered. 'But the only door is in the front.'

'Let's go in by the front door, just like we were invited,' Dehner suggested.

The two men advanced on the house. The smell of death became increasingly acrid. The two coyotes continued their feast, indifferent to the approaching humans.

Tom Laughton could take it no more. He picked up several large stones and heaved them at the animals. The coyotes retreated but not far. They would wait for the intruders to pass.

The sheriff and Dehner stopped to look down at what had been supper for the coyotes. Both men cringed in anguish. Laughton's face contorted. He mouthed the name 'Isaiah' to Dehner.

Rance patted the lawman's shoulder in a manner intended to comfort. The act seemed both absurd and desperately needed: a gesture of kindness in a man-made hell of grotesque savagery.

The detective drew his gun and stepped on to the porch. The wood was old and warped but didn't creak. Dehner noticed something for the first time. He pointed with his Colt toward the front window. It was broken. Only a few shards of glass lay underneath the window pane. The window had been broken from outside.

Dehner placed his hand on the door-knob, and pressed down on the lever slowly. Tom Laughton had now palmed his gun and was only a step behind the detective.

Inside, the horrible stench became heavier and slammed against them. Both men struggled to adjust to the obscene odour.

The visual scene was even more of an obscenity. Eleven coyotes had invaded the house and were ripping into four corpses that lay on the floor. Another animal was with them, and seemed to work in tandem as if an honourary member of the pack. Dark haired and wiry, the beast tore a pocket off the trousers of one of the dead bodies and hungrily picked up the coins that fell out.

'My God ... my God.' Tom Laughton's words of shock sounded almost like a prayer. The dark-haired beast was a man. The candle he had been carrying burned beside him, sweating hot wax on to the floor.

The man stood up and began to place the coins into his own pocket. Terror filled his face as, for the first time, he spotted the two men holding guns.

'Freeze,' the sheriff ordered.

The dark-haired man didn't obey. He screeched loudly and backed up, colliding with a coyote. The animal growled, revealing a mouth and teeth covered by blood. The coyote looked poised to attack the creature, who had knocked him away from the feast.

Laughton fired at the coyote. The animal gave a shrill yell as the bullet kicked it backwards. The animal again bared its reddened teeth. This time the coyote was fighting for survival.

The other animals scurried from the house. Most of them ran out the door, a few jumped out the window. Among those that went out the window was the dark-haired man. But as he ran, the thief had knocked over the candle which was now burning the pants of the corpse he had robbed.

Tom Laughton had a wounded coyote

and the start of a fire to contend with, Dehner would have to go after the thief himself.

As the detective ran from the house, he heard a second shot coming from Tom Laughton's gun and a final cry of pain from the coyote. Tom would have the fire out soon.

But Dehner had to concentrate on the thief who was now running at remarkable speed toward the stable. The man was not only fast, he was graceful, his movements like those of a deer. The detective remembered what Alice Cameron had said about the apple thief who invaded her home and terrified her daughter. 'His body seemed to be made of rubber.'

I think we've found Barbara's monster, Dehner thought.

Dehner was still several steps behind when the dark-haired creature ran into the stable. Dehner ran past the open double doors of the stable, and realized he had encountered a bit of luck. His quarry had tripped over something and was lying on his back, in front of a short line of stalls.

Rance's luck didn't hold. As he approached the fallen thief, Dehner was surprised by a hard kick to his head. The dark-haired man's leg had snapped upward like a long, vicious snake and hit its target.

The detective staggered backwards a few steps. When his vision cleared he saw that his opponent was on his feet. He circled around Dehner, like a boxer stalking an opponent.

'The name is Rance Dehner.' The detective spoke as his head turned, watching the strange creature that danced around him. 'I'm a detective. Sheriff Tom Laughton is with me. You can bet he's not far behind me. You'd be smart to surrender right now.'

'My name is Abe, like Abraham Lincoln!'

'Give up, Abe, this could be your — '

Abe charged at Dehner and delivered a fast punch to the side of his head. Dehner replied with a hard swing but Abe ducked down and danced backwards, completely avoiding his opponent's fist.

'Come git me, Mr Detective.' Abe had stopped circling Dehner and was now dancing backwards.

The detective knew why. A pitchfork was propped against the side wall his opponent was moving toward. Abe planned to deliver a few more rabbit punches to Dehner's head on their way to the wall. He would then grab the pitchfork and provide the coyotes with another meal.

The detective held both fists in front of his head. Abe seemed to have had formal instructions in boxing. Rance would have to play it Abe's way.

Or did he? Dehner realized he had committed one of the oldest mistakes in fighting. He had allowed his enemy to dictate the terms of the fight.

'You know, Abe, you haven't really committed any serious crime so far. We know you didn't kill those people. All you are guilty of is petty theft ... '

While he prattled on, Dehner slowly brought down his fists, making it appear to be a subconscious act. The ploy worked. Abe saw it as an opening and once again charged in. Dehner made a wild swing which Abe had anticipated. He ducked down, preparing to strike with an uppercut.

He never got the chance. Dehner swung his right leg and plowed his boot into Abe's jaw.

Abe hit the ground. He tried to get up but stumbled and hit the ground again.

'It's over,' Dehner shouted at his opponent. 'Don't make me hit you again, Abe. I will if I have to.'

Abe buoyed on to his knees and began to cry. Dehner thought that he should be disgusted with the spectacle in front of him. But, fight it as hard as he could, the detective felt some sympathy for a man who only a few moments before had been trying to kill him.

Perhaps it was Abe's face. Abe appeared to be a young man, mid-twenties probably, but his eyes looked glassy and confused. Those eyes were dominated by desperation and fear: the eyes of a man who was fighting to survive and losing.

But there was more. Abe's face reflected defeat: the face of a man who hadn't won even a minor skirmish in life's long series of conflicts.

Tom Laughton came running into the stable. 'Sorry I took so long, Rance.'

The detective kept his eye on Abe. 'That's OK, you had a wounded coyote to deal with and the start of a fire — '

'More than that.' Laughton dropped his voice to a low whisper as if he were in a confessional. 'The smell ... what the coyotes did to those bodies, I ... got sick.'

'I understand.' Dehner hastily changed the subject. 'Meet little Barbara's monster. His name is Abe.'

Tom Laughton's voice firmed up as he again assumed the role of lawman. 'Did you steal an apple from a little girl earlier in the day, Abe?'

Abe remained on his knees, looking up at Tom and Rance like a small boy explaining himself to adults. 'All I wanted was a bite. She shoulda shared with me.'

'Where are you from?' Tom asked.

'St Louis.'

'What did you do in St. Louis?'

'Took care of horses. I like horses and they like me. Mr Ungar, the man I worked for, paid for me to have boxing lessons. And not only lessons. I fought real fights, in front of lots of people. But something went wrong. I got hurt, had to stop boxing. But I could still take care of horses.'

Tom continued his questions. 'How did you end up in Arizona?'

'Mr Ungar had friends who were coming west on a wagon train, Mr and Mrs Dunford. They had a little boy, Charlie. They asked me if I would ride with 'em. Mr Dunford only had one arm. They paid for everything, so I did. Charlie and I were best friends.'

'Where are the Dunfords now?' Laughton suspected he already knew the answer to that question.

'They're dead. They all got the fever and died. Charlie, my best friend, died. He promised me he wouldn't.'

Abe began to cry. The two men left

him alone for a few moments and then Dehner resumed the questioning in a quiet voice. 'What happened after the Dunfords were gone, Abe? Did you stay on the wagon train?'

'I did for a little while.'

Dehner pressed on. 'Why for only a little while?'

'One night some men taught me how to play cards. I ain't never played cards before. I don't know nothing about betting. I ended up losing the wagon the Dunfords had bought. Lost everything. But the men let me keep one horse, anyhow. A saddle too. They were kind.'

Rance sighed deeply. He exchanged glances with Tom, before continuing his questions.

'After that, I guess you didn't stay with the wagon train, did you, Abe?'

'No. I just started to ride. I learned to break windows, that's how ya get inta places at night. But I never took much. It's OK to steal if you're hungry. Ain't that right?'

Abe looked upwards at the two men;

when they didn't reply to his question, his voice became more defensive. 'Now and then I find dead people. Men who got throwed by their horses, things like that. I take money outta their pockets. That ain't stealing. Dead people don't need no money.'

Neither Dehner nor Laughton saw any purpose in arguing with Abe. Tom spoke next. 'Did the smell bring you to this place?'

Abe appeared grateful for the neutral question. 'Yep.'

'Stand up, Abe,' the sheriff barked.

Abe obeyed. Laughton pointed to the only horse in the stable that was saddled. 'Is that your black?'

Abe nodded his head. 'Yep, it's the horse the men on the wagon train tole me to keep.'

'Do you know where Cooper is located?'

Abe began to sound more hopeful. 'Sure. I've been there.'

'The trail to Cooper is an easy ride. Even at night. You'll have to stop somewhere and camp out but you'll get there early tomorrow.'

'OK, Mr Sheriff.' Abe turned toward his horse. He was anxious to leave.

Laughton grabbed the man by his arm. 'Abe, when you get to town, look up Reverend Zack Peavy. You won't have trouble finding him. He lives in a house right next door to the church. Tell him all 'bout how you met me and Mr Dehner. Reverend Peavy will help you out. Understand?'

'Yep.'

'I know you've got some money.' The sheriff let go of Abe's arm. 'You can put your horse up at the livery and — '

Abe's face went red and his voice exploded like a child throwing a tantrum. 'The money's mine! Dead people don't need no money, taking money off dead people ain't stealing!'

Tom Laughton looked at the ceiling for a moment. His face also went red. The lawman wanted to yell but didn't. His voice was calm but carried an undercurrent of anger. 'No one called you a thief, Abe. You can keep the money. Now, what is the name of the man you have to look up when you get to Cooper?'

Abe heard the anger and didn't want to inflame it. 'Peavy. Reverend Zack Peavy. He lives in a house right beside the church.'

Laughton's reply was immediate and crisp. 'That's right. Now, I'll be back in Cooper soon, Abe. If I find you there but learn that you haven't seen Reverend Peavy, well, you're not going to be a very happy man. Understand?'

Abe nodded his head vigorously.

Tom pointed at the saddled black. 'Ride.'

Abe did what he was told. Tom and Rance stepped out of the stable and watched as the petty thief rode off.

'He's heading for the trail back to Cooper.' Laughton sounded satisfied.

Dehner wasn't satisfied. 'I hope Reverend Peavy has had experience with men like Abe.'

'He has.' The sheriff laughed and shrugged his shoulders. 'Cooper has two saloons and Reverend Peavy has provided the swampers for both of them. The reverend knows how to work with men who are ... simple ... he's good at finding ways for them to fit in.'

'Abe can be violent and he's fast with his fists.'

'Don't doubt it. But I'd rather have him in town where we can control him than have him out on the range, stealing from ranches and scaring little girls.'

Dehner realized what a fine sheriff the town of Cooper had in Tom Laughton. Laughton was young but with a mature mind that could handle the tough problems of being a western lawman. Difficult decisions had to be made on the spot and Laughton had the good judgement that was required. Once again, Rance thought back on his decision to give Andy Nolan a second chance. The detective hoped his judgement was as good as that of Sheriff Tom Laughton.

To Dehner's surprise, Laughton made a fist and pounded against one of the open doors of the stable. 'St Louis, the gateway to the west ... what a cruel joke!'

'What do you mean?'

'People come out here with their crazy notions of making a wonderful new life. Most of them end up like the Dunfords. People die on their way west, or they die trying to farm or start a ranch on a piece of worthless property.'

Tom Laughton was venting pent up emotions. Dehner spoke softly. 'Some people make it, Tom. They build a good life for themselves out here, far better than they could have had in the East.'

'Suppose so. Still, I wish those folks in St Louis, the ones who sell the wagons and all the supplies would be a bit more honest with folks. Not just talk about dreams. Let 'em know what's really in store for them.'

The sheriff looked at the ground; his face was covered by grief as he slowly lifted it to the sky. 'I knew them all.'

'You mean the people who were killed?'

'Yes. I told you 'bout the Burgesses and Isaiah. The two other bodies in the house belong to lawmen. Pete Tyler was a US Marshal. Amos Harrigan was a deputy. Both were fine men. I'll have to notify their people when we get back to town.'

There was nothing that could be said. Dehner didn't try.

Laughton's eyes left the sky. He stared straight ahead. 'There's a lantern in the stable. We'll need it. We've got five bodies to bury. We need to bury them deep. Then maybe we can get a little shut eye before we head out in the morning. I want to catch Ricky Cates. I want to catch him real bad.'

As they walked back toward the cabin, Dehner and Laughton saw that the coyotes were returning to their feast.

23

Cissy Runyan awoke at dawn. Instinctively, she crossed the barn to check on the Robin Hood of the Range. He was asleep.

She wanted to pretty up as she had promised her pa, but not in order to sell a horse. The girl returned to her special corner of the barn and reached into a far spot behind the bale of hay. She pulled out a copy of *Ricky Cates: The Robin Hood of the Range*, which lay right beside the Bible.

How could she be so blessed as to be able to help the Robin Hood of the Range? Would he ask her to go with him when he got better?

'I want that more than anything,' she whispered reverently to the dime novel.

Hoof beats sounded from outside. Cissy returned the publication to its hiding place, ran to the barn's double door and cracked it open. She immediately recognized one of the two riders approaching their house. The wiry man had to be Sheriff Tom Laughton. His aquiline profile was apparent even at a distance. Cissy had seen him in town a few times. The lawman had nodded, smiled politely and put two fingers to his hat. She had smiled and nodded back. That's as far as it went.

The other man was a stranger, at least to her. He was probably part of the posse that Laughton must have headed up, the posse that killed three innocent people and wounded Ricky Cates. Ricky had taken care of four of those fools. Maybe she could outsmart the two who were left.

The girl slipped out of the barn as she heard Tom Laughton shout, 'Hello, the house!' Her mother stepped timidly on to the front porch. Cissy couldn't hear exactly what the sheriff said next but from the few words she could pick up, he was apologizing for coming by so early. Cissy knew what the next question would be: Laughton would ask if he could speak to her husband. The girl also knew her mother's response.

'He's not feelin' well at the present, is there anything I can do?' Cissy had heard those words many times before.

As the girl got in close range of the house, the two men, still on their horses, turned to face her. Her mother raised her voice in a cheerful manner. 'This is our daughter, Cissy. Cissy, this is Sheriff Laughton and ... '

Laughton spoke up quickly. 'This here is Rance Dehner. He's a detective with the Lowrie Agency. They're sorta like the Pinkertons.'

Both men seemed so ... nice, Cissy thought. Maybe they believed they were doing the right thing when they opened fire on the Burgesses. Still, they were dangerous. She had to be careful. 'Nice to meet both of you. Hope you can stay a spell. Ma and me would be pleasured to fix you some breakfast.'

'Thank you, Miss Runyan,' the sheriff said as he patted his horse, 'but we hafta keep ridin', see — '

'What's goin' on?' Dencel stumbled on

to the porch and viewed the newcomers with hostility. 'What's the law doin' here? I ain't done nothin' wrong.'

'I'm sure you haven't, sir.' Dehner felt sorry for Iola. He had spotted the look of tension and fear on her face when her husband barged out of the house. He could only turn around and glance briefly at Cissy. Her reaction was harder to gauge. 'We're tracking a killer — '

'A killer!' Cissy's voice was almost a scream.

'Yes, ma'am!' the sheriff replied immediately. 'Ricky Cates robbed the bank in Cooper. He had a partner. Both Russ Adams and his wife were killed in the hold-up. We know Cates killed Shirley Adams. He also killed his partner, so he wouldn't have to split up the money. We're pretty sure he holed up at the Burgess ranch for a spell.'

'Oh . . . ' Cissy shook her head in a disjointed manner. She suddenly noticed the curious looks from the two lawmen. 'I mean, that makes sense . . . that he would hide out at a ranch.'

They're lying, the young woman thought to herself. They're lying in order to fool people into helping them catch the Robin Hood of the Range.

'Elsie and Simon Burgess paid a terrible price for hiding an outlaw,' Rance said. 'Two lawmen who stopped there were gunned down. Shot in the back. The Burgesses were both killed, as was a man who worked for them.'

Iola placed a hand on her chest. 'My Lord! That's horrible. You and the sheriff find that Ricky Cates, Mr Dehner, and see that he gets what's coming to him!'

'We intend to do just that. Thanks — '

Tom Laughton laughed softly. 'Looks like you've been up and busy doin' chores this morning, Miss Runyan.'

'Ah...' The girl shrugged her shoulders.

The sheriff pointed at Cissy's head. 'You've got hay in that pretty red hair of yours, Miss Runyan.'

Cissy hastily ran a hand through her hair, leaving the hay untouched. 'That's not so strange. See, I slept in the barn last night, takin' care of a sick horse. A pinto we hope to sell this afternoon ... '

Dencel shouted angrily at his daughter, as if she had insulted him, 'We ain't got no pintos!'

'Of course not!' Cissy again shrugged her shoulders. 'I meant to say a buckskin. I guess sleepin' in the barn made me dumber than a mule.'

'I know a little something about horses, like me to take a look at him?' Dehner asked.

'Obliged, but no ... not necessary ... he's just fine!'

'Well, Rance and I better be going.' The sheriff smiled at the three Runyans. 'Thanks for your time.'

As the lawmen rode off, Cissy spoke to her parents. 'There's a few more things that need tendin' to in the barn. Only take a few minutes, after that, I'll get helpin' with breakfast.'

Iola stared at her daughter for a moment before speaking. 'Honey, don't ya think it would be better if ya had something to eat first?'

'Leave the girl alone!' Dencel shouted

at his wife. 'She's got work to do at the barn. You get to makin' breakfast.'

Cissy watched her parents go back into the house before running to the barn. She slowed her pace as she got inside and approached the bales of hay. 'Mr Cates … Ricky?' she spoke in a stage whisper.

'It's me, Cissy.'

'You alone?'

'Yes.'

'You better not be lyin'.'

'I'd never lie to you, Mr Cates.' She approached the bales slowly. Peeking over them, she saw the outlaw holding a gun. 'You look just like you did the first time I saw you, Ricky Cates.'

'Who were those men?'

'I thought those riders would wake you up.'

'Who were they?'

'The law. Sheriff Laughton from Cooper and a range detective named Rance. Forgot his last name.'

'What did you tell them?'

The girl had originally planned to tell Ricky about her blunder concerning the pinto. But there was an undertow of anger in his voice and she wanted desperately to stay in his favour. 'I told them law dogs I hadn't seen hide nor hair of any stranger. You must be somewhere far off. And they believed me. They rode out of here fast, trying to pick up your trail.'

'Good work.'

'Could you put the gun away now, Mr Cates? I need to change your bandages, and...'

'Reckon, but be more careful this time.' The anger remained in his voice.

24

Dencel Runyan stood with his back to the barn, directly beside the door. He gripped the Henry in his hands as he listened to the conversation taking place inside. All his life, he had been cheated out of what was rightly his. Well, now he was going to get even with everyone. There had to be a reward of some kind out for Ricky Cates, but Dencel hoped for more. He hoped Cates still had the money from the bank hold-up.

He peered between the double doors and watched as Cissy moved around behind some bales of hay. That must be where Cates was hiding.

The girl looked around. 'Where did I put that bucket, I need — '

Moving faster than at any time in his life, Dencel ran into the barn, toward his target.

'Don't nobody move or I'll kill you!'

Dencel stopped when he could look down on Ricky Cates. The outlaw had partially yanked his gun from the holster that lay beside him. 'You drop that gun, or I'll take off your head.'

'Obey him, Mr Cates,' Cissy's voice was pleading. 'Please. My pa's a terrible man. He'll do it. He'll kill you.'

The look of savagery in Dencel Runyan's face convinced Cates that Cissy was telling the truth. He tossed his pistol into the hay behind him.

'Now you're bein' real smart.' Breathing heavily, Dencel moved behind the bales of hay and picked up the six-shooter. 'Just so you won't get no fool ideas.' Dencel gave Ricky a hard kick in the head.

'No, Pa,' Cissy screamed. 'He's already hurt bad.' The girl ran at her father. Dencel slammed his daughter on the side of her head with the pistol. She screamed again and dropped to the floor.

'You little tramp!' Dencel yelled down at her. 'You spent the night out here in the barn with this no good. I oughta...'

Dencel's eyes hit one of the back stalls.

'Well, well, whadda we got here.'

Cradling the Henry with his right arm and carrying Ricky's six-shooter in his left hand, Dencel made his way to the stall at the end of the row, where Sherwood was housed. 'So, you was tellin' some of the truth, anyway. This is a right fine pinto.' He spotted the saddle and saddle-bags that rested on the side of the stall.

He dropped both of the weapons to the floor and dug furiously into the saddle-bags. What he found there at first sent him into a stunned silence. The man's eyes went wide and he gave forth with a primitive cry of joy and harsh laughter.

Dencel flung the saddle-bags over his shoulder, retrieved the weapons and made his way back to his daughter. Cissy was crouched over Ricky Cates. 'Pa, that money is for poor people who — '

Dencel again made a loud, primeval laugh. 'Don't you worry 'bout that none. This money is gonna make one poor man very happy. Now, you saddle that pinto. I'm gonna pack me up a few things, and then I'm gonna ride far away from here.

I'll never have to look at you or your ma again.'

Iola entered the barn and looked about in a confused manner. 'I heard so much commotion — '

'You get back to the house, woman. Right now!' The look of savagery returned to Dencel's face.

His wife took a step forward, looking at her daughter. 'Honey, are you … '

Dencel pointed the six-shooter at his wife. 'Get back! Now!'

Terror covered Iola's face as she hurried from the barn. Seeing how effective the use of the pistol had been, Dencel pointed it at his daughter. 'You do as I say, girl.'

'Yes, Pa.' Cissy remained crouched over her patient as her father hurried from the barn.

Ricky Cates wanted to close his eyes and retreat into unconsciousness. The outlaw knew he couldn't do that. He had to come up with a good scheme, a plan which would get the money back and allow him to escape.

The killer remembered when he had rested under some trees after leaving the Burgess place. He had reloaded the Derringer and strapped it to his ankle in the event someone found him and took away his Smith & Wesson.

'Is your head feelin' any better at all, Mr Cates?'

Ricky Cates realized the Derringer wasn't his strongest weapon. His best weapon was Cissy Runyan. She was a weapon he would use.

'Hey now, what's with all this 'Mr Cates'? I thought you and me agreed to call each other by our first names.'

Cissy closed her eyes and started to cry.

'None of that, now.' Cates placed a hand on the girl's cheek. 'How are you feelin'?'

'Not so bad.' Cissy inhaled and quickly brushed away several tears. 'Pa hits me and Ma a lot. I was sorta expectin' him to do what he did. I ducked. I didn't get the full...'

Time was short and Cates didn't really care about Cissy's injury. He stroked her cheek. 'Cissy, last night I told you I'd only ask for one more favour. Guess I was lyin'. I got another favour to ask. A big one.'

'Sure. What is it, Mr … Ricky?'

'I need you to kill your pa.'

'What!'

Cates sat up slowly, lifted a pants leg and pulled out the Derringer. 'I can't get close enough to him for this gun to do much good. He'd be on his guard with me. But you can do it, Cissy. You can get close enough to kill him.'

The girl stared at the weapon in the killer's hand. Cissy had seen quite a few old rifles and knew how to handle them. But this gun was different. It looked sort of pretty, like something on a necklace.

'Aim for his chest, Cissy. That or his head.'

'I can't … he's my pa.'

'I gotta get that money back!' Cates paused, realizing he had to remain Robin Hood if his idea was to work. 'There's lots of poor folks who need the money.'

'I know, but … '

Heavy footsteps were approaching from outside, mixed with the sound of Dencel's manic laughter.

'Cissy, I've been doin' some serious thinkin' since we met up. I think we'd make a great team. I want you for my wife, Cissy. I love you.'

'And I love you.' She reached down and embraced Ricky Cates. The killer held her as tightly as he could and kissed her, not gently, on the lips. They parted as Dencel's laughter and shouts became dangerously close.

Cates lifted the Derringer toward the young woman. 'Before we can have a life together, you gotta do this one thing, Cissy. For us.'

Cissy's eyes briefly fell on her dress and the streaks of blood that were there: the blood of the man she loved and who loved her. Ricky Cates's blood had transferred on to her while they were kissing. The blood represented a sacred bond with the wounded hero who lay in front of her.

The girl nodded her head and took the gun.

25

Dencel stormed into the barn. The saddle-bags and a sack containing a few belongings were strewn over his shoulder. Ricky's Smith & Wesson was in his belt. He was carrying the Henry.

'Why haven't you saddled that horse, like I told you?'

'I'll saddle the horse.' Cissy walked around the bales of hay and began to approach her father.

'Well, get to it!'

'In my own time, Pa. There's somethin' I gotta do first.' She kept moving.

Dencel sensed that something very strange was happening but he didn't know what. 'I just gave your ma a goodbye beating. Maybe you need the same thing.'

Cissy was now only a few steps from her father. 'No, Pa.' The girl's face began to contort. 'You're not beatin' anybody again.' She lifted the Derringer and pointed it at his chest.

Dencel gave a loud, mocking laugh. 'I suppose your new amour, the thief, gave you that thing.'

Cissy's body trembled. She was having trouble pointing the gun straight. 'Don't you call Ricky Cates a thief! He's a finer man than you'll ever be.'

'You're talkin' crazy!'

'You're no kind of man at all,' Cissy shouted as the arm that held the Derringer began to shake. 'Beatin' up on women and demandin' your own way. That's all you've ever been good for.'

'I should kill you for sayin' that.'

'No ... no ... I'm the one who is gonna do the killin'. I'm gonna kill you for what you did to me and Ma. I'm gonna kill you for Ricky Cates, the finest man that ever lived.'

Cissy took a step closer to her father. Her entire body began to shake uncontrollably. The girl suddenly broke into tears, dropping the gun to the floor.

Dencel pushed the gun away with his foot as he slammed a fist into his daughter's jaw. The blow sent Cissy stumbling backwards. She tried to stay on her feet but collapsed to the floor.

A look of grotesque amusement appeared on Dencel's face as he looked down at his daughter. 'I guess that kick to the head I gave your boyfriend didn't do much good. Maybe I can kick some sense into you. It might take a few, but you ain't gonna be doin' no more talkin' about killin' your pa.'

Rance Dehner rushed into the barn and tackled Dencel Runyan. Both men hit the floor. The saddle-bags and sack fell from Runyan's shoulder but he still had the Henry. He gripped it with both hands and used it as a club, bringing it down on Rance's neck. Dehner delivered a hard punch to Runyan's throat, causing him to gasp for breath as he dropped the rifle and pushed Rance off.

Dencel grabbed the Henry and ran outside the barn. Dehner sprinted after him. When Dencel turned to fire the rifle, Rance was directly behind him and assaulted the large man with a whirlwind of punches. The Henry dropped to the ground, but Dehner deliberately didn't try to knock his opponent down. That would end the fight. Having witnessed what he had done to Cissy, Dehner wanted to inflict as much punishment on Dencel Runyan as he could.

Cissy staggered to her feet and looked out the barn door. Her father and the detective were still fighting, but the outcome wasn't in doubt. She hastily turned toward Ricky, who was on his feet but, like her, none too steady.

Ricky spoke in a loud whisper. 'Bring me the saddle-bags and the gun.'

Before carrying out the instructions, Cissy took another glance out the door. Her pa was on the ground. The Rance fellow was shouting at him to get up and fight some more. The girl smiled broadly. Pa didn't seem to care much for the notion.

The girl's playful thoughts quickly vanished. Both she and Ricky were in no shape to resist the law. The detective was pretty much in charge. But maybe that wasn't such a bad thing.

Cissy weaved a bit as she picked up the saddle-bags and the Derringer and carried them to Ricky Cates.

'That man who beat up on Pa, he's the detective I told you about. We can't get away from him, we're both too hurt.'

The man she loved didn't seem to be paying much attention to Cissy. He grabbed the saddle-bags and gun from her and immediately looked inside the bags.

'Ricky, surrender to the law. You never took too much money from the banks and you never hurt anyone. Not serious. Everyone knows you're a wonderful man. You'll only have to do a little jail time, a couple of years. I'll wait for you...'

The Robin Hood of the Range smirked and tossed the saddle-bags over his shoulder.

'Why, that's right sweet of you, girl. Before I turn myself in, why don't you give me one more kiss? Something to remember you by while I'm sittin' in a cold cell.'

The moment they kissed, Cissy knew this wasn't the Ricky Cates she loved. As soon as their lips parted, Ricky grabbed her by the hair as her pa had often done, held her against his chest and placed the Derringer at the side of her head.

'Ricky, please, you're … '

'Shut up and move. We're goin' outside. If you try to get away, I'll kill you.'

Ricky shouted as he paraded with Cissy toward the open barn door. 'Mr Detective, I know you're out there. You'd better be in plain view when I reach the doorway or Miss Cissy gets a bullet in her head. You hear me?'

'Don't harm the girl, Cates,' Rance's voice sounded from outside. 'You're holding all the cards. I'll do what you say.'

Cissy Runyan spoke in a whisper as she pleaded with her captor to release her. She fell silent as they left the barn and Ricky began talking to Rance.

'I got some orders for you, Mr Detective. Orders you better follow if you don't wanna see this girl's head come apart.'

'Like I said, Ricky, you're holdin' the cards.'

'First thing, I need me another gun. I believe that is a Colt .45 you got strapped on. Unbuckle the gun-belt and let it drop, real careful like, to the ground.'

Dehner needed to distract the killer. Tom Laughton was now advancing on Cates from behind. The sheriff had been hiding at the side of the barn.

Rance began to slowly take off his gun-belt. 'How do I know you won't use this gun to kill me? Or for that matter, to kill everyone here, like you did at the Burgess ranch?'

'You just don't know that, Mr Detective. Killing all those folks at the Burgess place did make things right convenient. People don't tend to cause much problems once they're dead.'

Ricky Cates gave a boisterous laugh. It would be his last laugh for some time. Sheriff Laughton grabbed the Derringer from the outlaw, spun him away from Cissy and delivered a hard roundhouse to the killer's head. Cates went down.

'Are you OK, Miss Runyan?' Tom Laughton asked as he handcuffed his prisoner, who was lying on the ground, semi-conscious.

Cissy nodded her head.

'You're not a very good liar, Miss Runyan,' Rance spoke as he picked up his gun-belt and began to buckle it around his waist. 'Tom and I knew something was wrong when we talked to you. But the land around here is so flat. Took us a while to circle back without being spotted.'

'We hid our horses when we got near the ranch, and split up,' Tom spoke as he stepped away from Cates and walked over to Dencel, who he also handcuffed. He picked up Cates's Smith & Wesson which had fallen on the ground during Dencel's fight with the detective. 'I took the house and Rance came here to the barn. Your ma is hurt, Miss Runyan, but she's gonna be OK. When I got here, Rance had your pa on the ground out cold. We heard some of your talk with

Cates. I hid by the side of the barn.'

'Thanks. Both of you. Obliged.' The young woman's words were flat and emotionless. Cissy's face was pale and her body limp, as if her soul had been ripped from her by force. She looked down at Ricky Cates. The killer's face was in the dirt, his hands cuffed behind him. Ricky Cates was alive, but to Cissy he was a lost dream.

'I wanted it to be true,' Cissy spoke to everyone and no one. 'Just this once, I wanted things to be good. Guess I wanted too much.'

The next thirty minutes or so were taken up with getting a buckboard ready to take the women and the two prisoners into town. The Robin Hood of the Range was the main catch, but Dehner was pleased that Tom Laughton planned to charge Dencel Runyan with assault and anything else he could throw at him.

The two women were withdrawn, speaking only when spoken to. They had been freed from one hell and seemed to wonder if another one awaited them.

Dehner noticed that Tom Laughton was very attentive to Cissy. The sheriff had appeared smitten by the young woman when he saw her earlier in the morning. Dehner hoped more would come of that.

As he checked on the two prisoners who were now lying on the flatbed of a dilapidated buckboard wagon, Dehner felt happy that Ricky Cates was alive. Who knows what nonsense those Eastern writers would have come up with if Cates had been shot down by a lawman or a detective? Now, those writers would be covering the trial of Ricky Cates and relishing all the details of Cates's murderous rampages. Ricky Cates would die at the end of a rope and the Robin Hood of the Range would already be dead.

26

Charlie scratched his grey beard as he settled into his familiar perch on the driver's bench of the stagecoach. Four men were standing on the boardwalk beside the coach. All four of them would have been content if Charlie had just waved and pulled away from the depot without saying a word, but Charlie could never resist performing for an audience.

'What's the name of that there outfit you work for, Mr Detective?' Charlie shouted.

'The Lowrie Agency,' Rance shouted back.

'I guess you're back in the good graces of Wells Fargo.' Charlie pointed with a thumb to the strongbox behind him. 'They'll be right happy when I get this money back — '

'You old fool!' Deputy Rollie Owens was doing the shouting this time. 'No sense in announcin' what you're doin' to the whole town.'

The deputy was right but Charlie wasn't about to admit it. 'Jus' cause you've been wearing a piece of tin for a hundred years don't give you no cause to order folks around! I got a right to speak my mind.'

'You also got the right to think before you speak,' Owens shot back. 'Maybe it's about time you started exercisin' that right!'

Charlie didn't have a reply to that. He sat quiet for a moment. He really didn't want to leave town quite yet. Finally, the driver looked at the young man who was riding shotgun beside him. 'You ready?'

'Yes, sir!' came the officious reply.

Rollie Owens laughed as the stage-coach rattled out of town. 'Poor Charlie. That kid they got ridin' shotgun with him is sure janglin' his nerves.'

Tom Laughton laughed along with his deputy. 'From what the doctor tells me Lou should be back on the job in a few weeks.' The sheriff turned his gaze to

Dehner. 'But I'll bet what Charlie said 'bout Wells Fargo is true. Those folks must be happy.'

Dehner nodded his head. 'After we got back into town yesterday with Ricky Cates, Dencel Runyan and the two Runyan ladies, I wired the Lowrie Agency in Dallas. A few hours later, my boss wired back with instructions from Wells Fargo. Yep, those folks are pretty happy.'

Rance Dehner was standing in front of the stage depot where he had made sure the money recovered from the stagecoach robbery was on its way back to Wells Fargo's main headquarters. Sheriff Tom Laughton and his deputy had accompanied him. While Charlie was boarding the coach, Reverend Zack Peavy had happened along. The four men now began to amble in the direction of the sheriff's office.

'Wells Fargo ain't the only happy ones,' Rollie declared. 'We got the money back in the bank and the folks in this town are a lot less ornery.'

'Who's going to run the bank, now that

Russ Adams is gone?' Rance asked.

'Russ's brother, William,' Laughton answered. 'He used to be a silent partner in the bank. He's not going to be silent anymore. William's going to take charge of the bank.'

'Yes.' Reverend Peavy's voice was robust. 'And he's already managing the bank the way his brother did. Dencel Runyan ran his ranch into a world of debt. The bank will take possession of the ranch but William will forgive the debts. Iola won't have to pay a thing. In fact, William plans on selling what few horses the ranch has and giving the money to Iola.'

The pastor smiled contentedly. 'The conversation I had with William this morning was quite uplifting. He told me his wife, Isabelle, is more than ready to run their hotel by herself.'

'That hotel is gonna be right busy,' Rollie said. 'The circuit judge will be by next week and we'll be tryin' Robin Hood. Newspaper people will be comin' here from everywhere.' Rollie turned to the pastor. 'What brings you out this mornin', Preacher, besides jawin' with William Adams?'

Reverend Peavy looked around Cooper, as if soaking in the town's return to normalcy. 'A pastor is like a lawman, Rollie. He does his rounds. My first stop is the livery.'

'Checking up on Abe?' the sheriff asked.

'Yes. So far, so good. Abe likes his job. He makes enough to provide for his needs and he gets to sleep there every night. I think it's going to work out.'

Deputy Owens took cigarette papers and a tobacco pouch out of his shirt pocket. 'Where you goin' after that, Preacher?'

'To see Carl Womack.' The pastor's eyes shifted to Tom Laughton. 'You know, Sheriff, shortly after you and Mr Dehner left town, Carl suffered a heart attack.'

Tom halted in surprise. The other men followed his lead. 'No!' The sheriff's voice got louder and his eyes bigger. 'No one told me Carl had a heart attack.'

Rollie stared at his unopened tobacco

pouch. 'Sorry, Tom, so much was goin' on yesterday, I plum forgot to mention it.'

The men resumed walking. 'Guess I shoulda figured something was wrong,' Laughton sighed as he spoke. 'I did notice that Etta was still running the store yesterday.'

'This town needs that store.' The pastor's voice took on a distant quality, the voice of a man who was thinking out loud. 'Dr Blaine says Carl should recover but it will take several months, maybe a year. I think I may have the answer here — '

Rollie was now scattering tobacco pieces on a paper. 'You claim to have the answer every Sunday morning, Preacher.'

'True enough, Rollie, but this is a different kind of answer. Carl Womack may have been a terrible acting sheriff but he's a good businessman. He can afford to hire people to run the store for him. I'm going to suggest he hire Iola and Cissy Runyan.'

Rollie barked a loud, appreciative laugh as the men halted in front of the sheriff's office. 'You do have the answer, Preacher!'

'Etta has been tending the store since Carl's breakdown; I've helped a bit. We can show Iola and Cissy the ropes.'

Tom Laughton pushed his hat back on his head and tried to sound casual. 'How are Cissy and Iola doing, Reverend?'

A look of intense concern waved over the pastor's face. 'As well as can be expected, I suppose. They've been through quite an ordeal. Both ladies feel bad about living with Etta and me. They think they're imposing. We're doing what we can to make them feel comfortable ... and wanted.'

Zack Peavy gave a slight smile and nodded goodbye before heading off for the livery. As the clergyman walked away, Rance Dehner realized he really had nothing left to do in the town of Cooper, Arizona. The realization left him a bit confused and sad. There seemed to be so many things that were not settled. But all of the unresolved issues could work themselves out without a detective from the Lowrie Agency. There was nothing more for him to do. The town no longer needed him. Rance's bay was tied up at the hitch rail in front of the sheriff's office; it was time to get on it and ride.

'No sense in me hanging around and getting in the way.' Dehner's voice was cheerful. 'I'm sure grateful to you gents for doing all the hard work on this case. Of course, I'll take all the credit once I get back to my boss in Dallas.'

There was the usual forced humour as the lawmen thanked Rance for his help. Sheriff Tom Laughton shook the detective's hand and gave a final 'So long', then turned to his deputy. 'I'll do a round. Why don't you stay here and keep an eye on things?'

'Sure, Tom.'

The sheriff walked off briskly. Dehner and Rollie watched him for a few moments. Rollie surprised Dehner when he spoke; the deputy's voice was almost paternal.

'He's headed for the preacher's house. He's sure taken with that Cissy Runyan. Not that I blame him, she's a fine girl. I

236

jus' hope Cissy realizes what a fine man Tom is. I guess what I'm really sayin' is, I hope she can see past that nose on his face.'

'I hope so, too.' Dehner patted Rollie on the back before mounting his bay. He rode past Tom Laughton as he left town. Rance waved goodbye to the sheriff, but Laughton didn't notice.

27

That night, while making camp, Rance Dehner thought about his long pursuit of Ricky Cates and the many people he had encountered in his efforts to capture the killer. What had made Ricky Cates the vicious outlaw he was? The detective pondered that question briefly while rubbing down his horse.

'Questions like that should have been asked long ago,' Dehner spoke in a sarcastic manner to his bay. 'By the time I got together with Ricky, he was a little past the point where he could be reformed.'

After making sure his horse was taken care of, Dehner began to collect tinder in order to build a fire. He remembered some of the nights he and Sam Wilcock would make camp together. No one could build a fire quicker than Sam.

As Dehner got a fire started he wondered if he would end up like Sam

Wilcock. A man who was totally uncon-
nected to anyone except for his job; a
man who seemed to break down when
one careless misstep caused him to fail
at his duty and appear to be a fool.

A cold wind began to twirl around him,
and sparks from the fire shot in his direction. Dehner tried to think of happier
notions as his coffee heated up. He hoped
Cissy Runyan would realize what a fine
man Tom Laughton was, or as Rollie put
it, 'see past that nose on his face'.

But Cissy had been raised by a brute
of a father and betrayed by Ricky Cates.
Could she ever really trust another man
again?

Rance looked upwards. The black sky
appeared to be in an uncontrolled spin,
as if telling him the whole universe was
broken, and it was his job to patch up
what cracks he could find here and there
and be on his way.

The detective suddenly understood
the reason for his melancholy. He really
cared about Tom, Cissy, and many of the
other people he had encountered while

on Ricky Cates's trail. He thought of them as friends, but they were friends he would probably never see again.

Of course, this wasn't the first time he had experienced such a yearning. He reckoned it came with the job.

Dehner wondered if he should quit the Lowrie Agency and find himself a job as a lawman in a town somewhere like Cooper, Arizona. He could become part of a community. Maybe even ...

A fresh wave of sparks came at him. Hell seemed to be mocking him and once again he was engulfed in that terrible day. The day when he had been a lawman in a town similar to Cooper, Arizona, a day when he had found the woman in his life, a woman he loved with a magnificent passion. But like Sam Wilcock, he had made one foolish misstep. Only, his mistake had been tragic and the woman he loved had died because he failed.

The detective eyed his saddle-bags. He usually carried two books with him, a Bible and a book of plays by Shakespeare. Rance Dehner would do a lot of reading on this night. He would feel connected to the people and ideas on the pages he read.

And for a short while, he would feel he belonged.

We do hope that you have enjoyed reading this large print book.

Did you know that all of our titles are available for purchase?

We publish a wide range of high quality large print books including:
Romances, Mysteries, Classics
General Fiction
Non Fiction and Westerns

Special interest titles available in large print are:
The Little Oxford Dictionary
Music Book, Song Book
Hymn Book, Service Book

Also available from us courtesy of Oxford University Press:
Young Readers' Dictionary
(large print edition)
Young Readers' Thesaurus
(large print edition)

For further information or a free brochure, please contact us at:
Ulverscroft Large Print Books Ltd.,
The Green, Bradgate Road, Anstey,
Leicester, LE7 7FU, England.
Tel: (00 44) **0116 236 4325**
Fax: (00 44) **0116 234 0205**